Sandrine's
Letter
to
Tomorrow

Sandrine's Letter to Tomorrow

DEDRA JOHNSON

PUBLISHING

Brooklyn, New York

Please direct inquiries to:

Ig Publishing
392 Clinton Avenue
Brooklyn, NY 11238

Library of Congress Cataloging-in-Publication Data

Johnson, Dedra.
  Sandrine's letter to tomorrow / Dedra Johnson.
     p. cm.
  ISBN-13: 978-0-9788431-2-0
  ISBN-10: 0-9788431-2-6
  1. African American girls--Fiction. 2. New Orleans (La.)--Fiction. 3.
United States--History--1969---Fiction. I. Title.
  PS3610.O3364S26 2007
  813'.6--dc22
                                    2007033180

To my family

1

I woke up panting, thinking that when Dad pulled up to the curb to take me to his mother's for the summer, Mama would tell him I wasn't going because she'd found dirt on top the kitchen cabinets and paper wasp nests in the eaves of the porch. I'd spent the few days I'd been out of school cleaning every part of the house I could think of, cigarette butts and shiny square wrappers under Mama's bed in the front room, ashes and water rings off the windowsills and sticky fingerprints on the panes, mouse droppings and roach legs behind the stove, and though I was sure I'd swept the concrete porch as clean as the kitchen, I felt ready to jump out of my skin to check. Mama had never stopped me from spending the summer with Mamalita, but the chill at the back of my neck told me anything could happen and I'd woken up too many times smelling Mamalita's house and feeling her skinny fingers pulling my hair into cornrows to let a single wisp of dust keep me in New Orleans all summer.

The heavy dark blue and green plaid curtains kept out the heat and sunlight except for a corona around the edges, enough light for me to check my suitcases by the bedroom door, my clothes for the five-hour drive neatly folded on top, sandals set primly side by side near the door. Last night, one of Mama's friends stayed over, but I hadn't been woken by their voices or the screen door slamming as he left early and I listened at the door before I opened it and tiptoed to the kitchen. I got all the rags and sponges I used for cleaning from the bucket under the sink, some smelling like bleach, others of nose-burning ammonia, and turned the faucet on slow, letting the water dribble until they were all wet. I pulled out the white three-step stool, got onto the counter and wiped the top of the white cabinets up near the ceiling, wobbling on my tiptoes, hoping I didn't fall not because it might hurt, but because it might wake Mama and her friend and get me yelled at for either being awake or not having cleaned the top of those cabinets in the first place.

One of them coughed. I tried to move fast but quiet and didn't have time to rinse the rags and sponges, all dark gray from dust so thick it rose up in curls and little balls.

I was in my room and had just pulled the faded pink sheet over my shoulders when I heard voices, footsteps in the hall and then the screen door slam. Then Mama was in my room, tapping one bare foot, tying her white and yellow robe closed. I knew she wasn't wearing anything underneath; one dark brown leg slipped out of the robe, bare all the way up without the shorts she slept in when no friend stayed the night.

"Lift that curtain some so I can see," she said. With a clothespin I kept on the windowsill, I folded it up a third of the way and the strong light glared off the wood floor. She picked up the biggest suitcase.

"I already packed, Mama, see?" I said.

I pulled my legs out of the way just as she swung the suitcase onto the bed. "I'll see myself about that," she said. She opened the suitcase and started tossing everything out onto my legs, neatly folded t-shirts, shorts and cutoffs, a pair of Toughskins jeans for protection from match-head-sized ticks in the country, tennis shoes, good white sandals wrapped in wax paper, and three dresses for church folded flat and wide to cut down on wrinkles. Mama undid all my careful folding and arranging without a word, wink or whistle.

"When's he gonna be here?" Mama said.

"Eleven o'clock, I think."

She took two more dresses out of my closet and repacked the big suitcase, folding quick and fast. "I don't want him coming in the house, you hear?" She clicked the big suitcase shut then flung open the smaller one, a disgusted frown on her face though I had made neat layers of panties, baby doll pajamas, a nightgown, a few pairs of socks, a book and two Barbie dolls I'd packed in case it rained; I didn't need much else because usually I read, helped Mamalita, played in the yard or with the kids down the dead-end street, something neither Mamalita nor I ever told Mama about. Mama tossed out the books and Barbies, permanently I thought, until she dumped all the clothes out and started refolding my clothes into thirds instead of the halves I'd done.

"And . . ." I stopped in the doorway, my clothes for the drive still on the floor where they had fallen off when Mama picked up the suitcases; I tucked the clothes under my arm. "You keep your mouth shut. He asks you about me or this house you just say 'fine,' hear me?" When I left, she was muttering, "He don't want live with me, he don't get to know what goes on in *my* goddamn house . . ."

Before I went to the bathroom to get dressed, I passed through the front room, our living room and Mama's bedroom, to look out the front door at the eaves of the porch. Clean. The whole room smelled musty, sweaty and sharp sour, Mama's clothes from yesterday thrown across the sofa, empty cans of Jax beer and an overflowing frog-shaped ashtray crowding the three framed pictures on top the console tv. One was my first grade picture, all front teeth missing from my wide smile, the one in front of Mama with one of her friends, Joe Henry, their eyes half-closed, the tiny table in front of them covered with empty glasses and little red straws. The third, pushed toward the back, I only got to look at closely when Mama wasn't in the room; if she saw me with it, she'd take it from me and send me to my room or to do dishes. It was a Polaroid, too small for the brass-colored frame, the colors blurring but I could still pick out Mother Dear, Mama's mama, my aunts and uncles and my mother, all still teenagers, except Tamira, waist-high to Dear. Uncle Jerry stood in the back, taller than Uncle Frank though Uncle Frank was three years older, Aunt Margie, Auntie Z and Mama in front with Tamira but it was the white lady next to Dear, her hand on Mama's shoulder, I couldn't figure out. Social worker? Teacher? In a family picture? My stomach hurt I was so hungry. I put the frame down to go get dressed.

Light came in the kitchen from the east through the three big windows, the off-white counters with pale-colored speckles reflected the light, the cabinets were white and smudge-free— I'd scrubbed them every morning with Mr. Clean and Comet for the fingerprints and wiped them once more each afternoon before Mama got home—and the pale blue and white tile was clean from corner to corner, even along the baseboards and in the crevices of doorways. While I crunched through a bowl of corn flakes, I heard Mama talking outside, her voice light and happy; she must've been talking to a neighbor since no "friend" of hers came by during the daytime, or at least this early, not with Mother Dear next door watching. When Dad called, her voice was annoyed and low, with Mother Dear it was fast and high-pitched but not happy and with me she was all that and more—flat and slow, tired and clipped, and, late at night, drawling and sour with beer.

Mama sat on a folding chair on the porch, looking out at the street. It was hot and humid early. None of the kids on the block would be out to play until late, between dinner and complete darkness, when it got cooler and there might be a little breeze. My suitcases were right inside the screen door. I sat on the top step to put on my sandals, huaraches Mama had bought from a man around the corner who made them in his shed. I hadn't worn them much yet and the leather straps were stiff.

"Get up," Mama said. "What are you wearing?"

I stood so she could see my blue t-shirt with a US flag on front and the cut-off shorts she'd made from last year's jeans. One of her friends Dave had given me the t-shirt, said he bought it from a van on St. Bernard and when I tore it from the plastic bag, brand new, she pouted at Dave, "You ain't get me one?" I hadn't worn it yet to keep from ruining it with Mr. Clean and Comet and bleach.

"Go change." I opened my mouth to ask why I had to change for a five-hour car ride, some through red dust it was too hot to close the windows against, but Mama raised her hand at me, as if to block me from sight. "You will not go with him looking like some project orphan. Go put on a dress. And your good sandals, not those back-alley huaraches."

I wanted to let the screen door slam behind me but she already sounded tight and mad. Dad had been coming to get me for the summer ever since they split up and though I don't remember the first summer pickups when I was three and four, I could guess what they had been like by how things were now and how I felt the closer it got to Dad showing up. Mama always had my suitcases outside on the porch or right inside the screen door and the closer Mama stood to the porch steps, the guiltier and jumpier I felt. It seemed like I had done something wrong when she waited inside, looking through the screen door at my back, but if she stood behind me while I waited on the steps, her face hard like she couldn't wait for me to leave, I felt like my head would bust open. One year, she threatened to make me wait in my room because she didn't like how I waited on the porch for him, like I'd been waiting since last summer she said. I didn't say anything back but later, a little while before Dad was due, I told her she was the one who always wanted me to wait on the porch. She looked at me funny and said she didn't know what I was talking about.

The only short-sleeved dress left in the closet had penny-sized sunflowers on puckered white that looked like seersucker but was thicker and hotter to wear, with a yellow ribbon I had to reach behind to tie, closing my eyes so my fingers could see. The puckers looked pretty in the mirror but the inside was scratchy, the puckers held in body heat, and the white and yellow made my barely-the-color-of-teacakes skin look even paler. The Sundays I had to wear this dress, the girls from school I saw, the amber and cinnamon and chocolate girls, rolled their eyes at me and scooted away if I sat nearby, like they would catch it. Mama told me all the time I was no better than anyone else, especially her, even if my skin was "white," no matter what Dad said, she'd add, though Dad, and Mamalita and his brothers and sisters, never told me or anybody they were better. A girl with the most beautiful chocolate skin and the prettiest ribbons and ponyknots for her hair that matched our red, gray and white plaid skirts at school had decided in second grade, like Mama, that all light black people thought they were better than darker ones, though the girl had never talked to me and I wasn't sure of her name since I had been skipped. She yelled at me while we were lining up after recess or lunch or Mass, as if finishing an argument, "You might think you white but you ain't" and all the girls and boys looked over and frowned or rolled their eyes in agreement. When I told Mama, she said, "She wouldn't accuse you of being stuck-up if you wasn't." I wasn't stuck up and I wasn't white. My features were the same as the darker girls, just covered with lighter skin and when Dad came for me each summer, I felt a certain relief. At Mamalita's, every neighbor child was a different color, even in the same family, and nobody said anything about my skin. I stayed outside in the sun as much as I could, until it got too hot or Mamalita coaxed me into the shade with watermelon or ice cream or peas to shell, and though I was smarter than some of the kids, it had nothing to do with skin. White people thought those kinds of things, that skin color made you smarter, better. I was never going to think like a white person. At least not like they thought about black people.

"He's here."

Mama didn't have time to retie my ribbon or make me change my sandals. I ran out and thought about the screen door after it slammed behind me but Dad's arms were around me, my arms were around his neck, and his scratchy kiss tickled my ear. He wasn't in his two-seater but a long green Pontiac I'd never seen before. When he put me down and I looked back, Mama was already inside and though it was hard to see through the dark screen into the dim house, I hoped she was waving.

• • •

We went to the K&B a few blocks from my school. The soda fountain was against the front window, the view outside blocked by purple K&B signs painted on the glass and it smelled like sugar had been sprayed in the air. At the end of the counter closest to the door sat Philipa and her daughter Yolanda. Dad hadn't told Mama, at the house, or me, in the car, that Philipa and Yolanda were in town, too. I couldn't believe Philipa's love-seat-sized butt fit on a purple-topped stool. She wore a bright yellow shirt and skirt on her wide body and looked like a lemon with a caramel stuck on top. Last summer, they had been at Dad's apartment most of the nights I spent there. Yolanda and I had had to make our bed of sofa and chair cushions and in the mornings I'd looked scarred, my face covered with red itchy-looking crosshatches while Yolanda's chocolatey skin hid the grooves on her cheeks and in her dimples.

Yolanda hopped down, looking as excited as I'd felt when we walked in. Philipa smiled a little, took Dad's hand and started walking with him to the door. I looked back at Yolanda's empty soda glass on the counter and smelled root beer on her breath.

The Pontiac was Philipa's car. Yolanda told me that and more—that she was living with her mother now for good and didn't just visit in summer anymore, went to the last few weeks of school but she'd be going somewhere else in September, hoped I brought all my Barbies so we could play after camp. I wasn't going to camp, I never went to a camp, I went to Mamalita's when Dad was working, Philipa or no Philipa. When Yolanda was talked out, we played cards—crazy eights and go fish and pitty pat.

• • •

The block looked new, the curbs and curb cuts whitish like they had finished drying that morning. Each townhouse was shaped the same, with the same false shutters on the first floor windows and tiny false balconies on the second floor windows, but with a different pale color on the trim—pale green, pale blue, pale teal, pale yellow and a pink that was almost white. Dad's little black sports car sat in the driveway of the pale-green-trimmed townhouse at the end of the street where the pavement stopped and trees, bushes and leggy dandelions grew thick.

For the first time since leaving the house in New Orleans, Dad smiled. He rubbed the hood of the Fiat. "We'll go for a ride later," he said in a low voice to me.

"Oh, goody, a ride in the car!" Yolanda said on her way into the house. There was no way she was going. It was a two-seater, there was no room, and he hadn't been talking to her anyway.

"Come on, honey," Philipa said to me. She stood by the open trunk and I went to help. I picked up the small suitcase with my books and toys inside. Something bumped the back of my head. "Get the other one too," said Philipa, "I ain't your maid." Then she gave me a big smile and walked away, into the townhouse. I felt dizzy, not sure if I'd heard her right.

Inside felt like a motel—the furniture, the carpet, the paint on the walls, the lamps, the handrail on the stairs all looked brand-new, like it was their first day there, too. The first floor had a living room with the chairs, sofa and TV arranged in a box, a patch of carpet with a glass dining table and four chairs made of gold-colored metal tubes and seats that looked like rattan, a narrow kitchen. On the wall by the stairs hung pictures of Dad in his cap and gown, Dad with Philipa, and all three of them together, the pictures of them so new they were shiny without any glass over them.

Yolanda helped me drag the suitcases up the stairs. "Here's our room," she said. Everything looked new there, too. Yolanda had a few toys in the closet. Two dresser drawers and half the closet were empty. "Did you bring any Barbies?" Yolanda said.

"Uh-huh." My stomach was so empty I could taste it. "I'm hungry."

"We could have Froot Loops," Yolanda said.

We ran down the stairs and the running was so fun we

giggled our way to the kitchen. The bowls were in the top cabinets, the cereal on top of the refrigerator. "A chair," I said.

"Not that one!" Yolanda said. "Uncle Tony sits in that one and Mama sits in that one."

I gripped the cold metal arm of the third chair and had it halfway to the kitchen when I heard Philipa and Dad thud down the stairs. He wore navy pants and an undershirt, smoking another cigarette, Philipa a tent-like flowered duster that reminded me I was still in the dress Mama made me wear.

"Put that chair back," Philipa said.

"We were hungry," I said. "I was going to get some cereal."

"Come sit with me, cream pie," Dad said as he sat in the chair I held. It felt like I had waited all year to sit in his lap. "Do you like it here?" he said.

I hadn't been there long enough to tell. I said, "Yeah," and he smiled again so I guessed I'd said the right thing.

"Phil?" Philipa stepped closer. He smiled at me again and said, "So this, this is your new mama. What would you like to call her?" and Yolanda peeked around her, grinning so hard her eyes were almost squeezed shut. "Call her Mama, too," Yolanda said. I could feel Dad waiting. I felt like everyone had been talking about, planning and waiting for this but no one had thought to tell me. I couldn't think of anything to call her but Fatty or Miss Phil. I knew what he wanted. Even thinking about calling her Mama made me feel cold and shaky, like I had no mother and Philipa was all I'd ever have.

"Okay."

Dad hugged me, a cozy hug I could've slept in. "Phil and Yolanda will get you settled in," he said. "I'm working tonight. I'll be gone by the time you wake up in the morning," he added when I looked at him.

He went back upstairs. I sat in the warm chair, stomach soured by emptiness. Philipa came out the kitchen with a cigarette. I didn't think she would let me stand on a chair to get a bowl.

"Well," said Philipa. "What to call you."

"Sandrine."

"Sandrine has got to be one of the ugliest names I've heard in a long time," Philipa said. "Your mother must've picked that out."

"Sandi!" said Yolanda. " 'Cause she's sandy-colored."

"Dry sand, for sure; wet sand looks like blackface next to her. What's the rest of that name of yours?"

"Sandrine Antonietta Cecelia—"

"Mama, we're hungry."

Philipa bustled to the door to kiss Dad goodbye, her hips bouncing like beach balls under the duster and I wanted to laugh. Over her head he winked at, I thought, just me but Yolanda ran to kiss him, too. Then he was gone. Philipa smiled until we couldn't hear the Fiat anymore. Then she stretched and yawned.

"Mama," said Yolanda, "we're hungry."

"Make a sandwich," she said.

"Can we have Froot Loops?" I said.

"No!" On her way up the stairs she said, "There's some jelly, some bologny, bread . . ." The bedroom door slammed, weakly because every door sounded hollow and made of cardboard. She turned up the TV and we could hear it everywhere in the town-house and even on the stoop where we ate the sandwiches I made, two bologna sandwiches and two jelly sandwiches. When I bit into the jelly sandwich, the Ann Page grape jelly tasted like watery sugar and I missed the homemade, light orange jelly Mamalita made out of pomegranates, thinly spread on a biscuit, a snack on the back stairs when the kids down the street had to go in for chores or because one of the small ones started crying. I let Yolanda eat the rest.

We played on the stoop with my two Barbies and Yolanda's Barbie and Ken until dark. The streetlights floated pale green in a black sky and the bugs in the trees at the end of the street were power tool loud.

"What time do we have to go to bed?" I said. Yolanda shrugged. "You don't have a bedtime?"

"It's summer. And camp don't start 'til Tuesday."

"Doesn't. I'll be at Mamalita's."

"You're not going to Mamalita's."

"Yes I am."

"Mama said you was going to camp with me."

"Were. And I don't go to camp."

"You don't want to stay in here by yourself all day. You get bored. Scared . . . Dad used to leave me in the apartment all day. Even when I was little. Mama told him he had to put me in school or something. Mama says he's not coming back ever . . . I don't listen to her," she said with a pout. I was confused until I remembered Yolanda's father, somewhere in Washington, D.C. or Boston.

My stomach still bubbled and griped. We changed for bed, turned out the light and opened a curtain so the streetlight glowed in, coloring everything pale green, even our skin, and though Yolanda looked like a jewel, my skin absorbed the light and looked alien green.

• • •

Dad worked every day, even Sunday. He said he worked at two clinics deep in the country and was the only doctor. He told me the names and I wanted to look in an atlas but they had no atlas or maps, no encyclopedias, no dictionary, no books I could find. The first thing Yolanda and I did in the morning after we opened our eyes was check their door. If it was open it meant they were both gone and there might be some bacon or ham left from the breakfast Philipa cooked. But if it was closed, Philipa or Dad or both were sleeping and we had to be quiet and I'd make toast and jelly even though I hated that watery jelly.

Yolanda sat in the open front door, elbows on knees, Barbie dangling by the hair from her hand. I sat down quietly behind her and opened the book I'd brought with me, *A Wrinkle in Time*. I read the folded-over page without recognizing anything. Trying not to make noise with the pages, I went backwards, reading the first few lines on each page until I found something I knew I'd read before. I'd tried reading since I'd been there but Yolanda asked every few minutes if I was done yet, did I have to read it for school, make her a sandwich, she can't find her Barbie, why was I reading? I had tried reading it to her but she'd started talking about Barbies after a page, like she hadn't heard or understood anything I'd read.

The sun was blocked and I looked up, Yolanda standing in the doorway with one hand on her hip. Through her legs I saw dark legs in shorts outside, and a bat swinging down past the legs. I waited for the smack of a ball on the bat but just heard laughs, including Yolanda's.

"Shut up, motherfuckers!" a boy said. "You! Shut up."

Three of the boys stood in a triangle in the middle of the street, yelling, laughing and taunting all at once. The tallest one was the color of dark caramels and wore clothes that looked dusty and worn out like somebody had worked in them. He made a few practice swings with the bat and spit toward the boy pitching.

"He's cute," Yolanda said. I looked again. He looked like any other boy to me, his nose a little narrower than some other boys, his head longer because he was taller and probably older. "Mama would say he was cute," she said. He missed the next swing and the jeering got louder. He looked our way and Yolanda waved. She turned her smile to me. "See?"

"See what?"

"You don't like boys?" She sounded like girls at school, a question meant as an insult because any answer was wrong. "Boys are fun," Yolanda said. "Unc—I mean, Daddy says I have to wait but Mama says when I'm eleven, I can go for pizza and stuff. She said she went on her first date when she was twelve." I opened my book and hung my head low over it.

The door slammed. Yolanda ran to the living room window, low and wide like a motel one, and peeked out. I went to look, too. Philipa's green Pontiac stopped a few feet from the boys. The younger ones moved right away but the tall one, bat on his shoulder, looked awhile at Philipa's car before he slowly lowered the bat and stepped back just enough for the car to pass. After Philipa parked in the driveway and hoisted herself out, she leaned on the car to watch the tall boy and the short one pitching step back into the street. The tall boy hit the ball into the empty field across from the townhouses and all the shorter boys ran to find it in the long grass and trash. Philipa spoke to the tall one while he waited and she came inside with a big smile on her face.

"He says his name is Malachi but the boys call him Mike." She peeked out the curtain above us. "You can go watch him if you want." Yolanda ran to the front door. "And stay inside this house, hear?" Philipa said. I sat in one of the big chairs and opened my book again.

"How old is he, Mama?" Yolanda said from the open doorway.

"He didn't say. Fourteen, I think."

Philipa stood over me, hands on her hips. "You better go look before he goes home," she said.

"I've seen boys play ball before," I said.

She walked away laughing and I felt hot and embarrassed, not sure why she wanted me to look at some stupid boys. Yolanda bounced from foot to foot, looked back to see where Philipa was, then swayed back and forth on her feet, a half-smile on her face ready to break open.

• • •

I finished *A Wrinkle in Time* and read it again. Mamalita would take me to the library every week but no one had mentioned it here, I hadn't seen one on our way through town, and Yolanda, when I asked, looked so confused, like she didn't know what the word "library" meant, I wanted to hit her. I was tired of Yolanda all day. It was more like babysitting than having a friend to play with and the babysitting just made me mad since I was only a year or so older and had no business watching her all day, like that's why they brought me, not to see Mamalita or Dad.

In the downstairs closet behind the vacuum and broom I found some medical books, Dad's, in a plastic milk crate. There was one old book from Mamalita's house, brown, a little mildew-smelling, and I started reading it, my legs folded under me. It was a *Little House on the Prairie* book I'd read twice already at Mamalita's and I didn't pay much attention to what it said; the books were simple-minded and boring, but it was better to have words in my head and eyes than nothing. I shoved the vacuum aside and slammed the broom against the back wall to sit on the books. The light bulb was yellow but bright enough to read by.

The door opened. Yolanda stood there wiggling her toes, carrying the Barbies by their hair. She saw the book and sucked her teeth, stood there another half-minute and sucked her teeth again. When I didn't stop reading, she drifted away. I crossed my legs and leaned back on the cool wall. I could hear humming from the air conditioning and low-pitched shouting outside. Yolanda, out of my sight, said, "It's Mike and some boys," and walked past the closet door. I heard the deadbolt scrape open and saw light cut across the carpet. I expected to hear a ball hit or more shouting, but a car door closed, a motor revved and Yolanda called "Sandi!" I peeked around the closet door. In the bright bleached outside was a long convertible, white and chrome, and Yolanda sat on the passenger door, her bare feet dangling over the street. Mike leaned into the car, talking to the driver who looked a lot older than Mike. The driver, the collar of his white shirt wafting up when the wind got strong, had his arm draped over the car door. Yolanda waved both arms wildly.

I sat and closed the closet door. I still heard the motor. Then a woman yelled, doors slammed and the car drove away. The closet door jerked open and a woman with dark skin but gray eyes and white hair looked down at me, one hand on her hip. She smiled.

"And you're in here reading a book," she said, shaking her head just a little. "Come on out here. I'm Miss Augustine. I live right down the street in the pink townhouse. And you, Little Miss Hot Stuff," she said to Yolanda, who she held tight by the wrist, "almost ended up in more trouble than you can even guess at."

Miss Augustine's head swiveled around as she looked the townhouse over. She looked in the refrigerator, still holding on to Yolanda who leaned as far away from her as she could. All we had was the heel parts of a loaf of bread, an almost empty jelly jar, one slice of ham that had gotten hard on one side, and an empty milk gallon. Philipa had said that morning she'd bring home food but I didn't tell.

"You girls come with me," she said. "We'll have some lunch and you can help me in my yard."

"We not supposed to leave the house," Yolanda said with a smug grin.

Miss Augustine pulled Yolanda close to her face and said, "But you can sit in a car with boys three times your age from you don't know where?" She smiled at me and offered her other hand. "Let's go, girls. It's already after two, you must be hungry. You can bring your book. What's your name?"

"Sandi," Yolanda said.

"Sandrine," I said. "And she's Yolanda."

We walked past the yellow and teal-trimmed townhouses into the pink-trimmed one. Miss Augustine's inside walls and even the rail on her staircase were cotton candy pink. I could still smell the bacon she must've fried for breakfast. Instead of a sofa, she had three big chairs and matching footstools; instead of a dining table she had a long wood table with two benches, like a polished picnic set. Glass shelves near the staircase had ceramic and glass things covering all the shelf space—fancy eggs, riots of color with lots of gold trim and on stands that looked like gold thimbles; little brown-skinned shepherds and shepherdesses; a few Virgin Marys and Jesuses, including a Black Virgin Mary; cats sleeping; a dog with a stick in his mouth. On the walls she had an old map of the United States, before Hawaii and Alaska, and a painting of a dim, drippy bayou. It was cool and quiet inside.

After she locked the door and put the key in her pocket, Miss Augustine let go of Yolanda who jumped away and rubbed her wrist. Miss Augustine told us to sit down at the picnic table and disappeared into the kitchenette. Yolanda stuck her tongue out at the wall Miss Augustine was behind. We heard pots clang onto the stove, water pouring.

"My girls'll be home later today," Miss Augustine said. "They go to Tougaloo."

I hunched my shoulders and laughed into my hand at the name. "What's a toogaloo?" I said to Yolanda who pouted her lips out like a frog and dropped her head on the table. I poked and poked and all she would do was sigh.

"Miss Augustine?" Yolanda's head popped up and she screwed up her face to give me a mean look. "What's a toogaloo?"

"A college."

Yolanda folded her arms and turned away from me. "Mama's gonna be real mad at you," she said.

"I wasn't the one sitting in a car with boys."

"Mama's not gonna care about that. This . . . " She pointed to the table and nodded over and over, her big eyes staring at me.

Sizzles and pops came from the kitchen and soon we smelled frying chicken. "Shut up," I said. I was hungry. No one had cooked for me since I left New Orleans. Philipa cooked only if Dad was home, awake and hungry, which had only happened at breakfast before we woke up. "Your mama doesn't care what happens to us," I said.

"Yes she does!"

Miss Augustine filled the table—potato salad, fried green tomatoes coated in flour and pepper, crispy fried chicken wings, white bread, sweet tea, green beans cooked with little chunks of ham. The tomatoes were peppery and tart; Yolanda spit hers out on her plate.

"You like that book? *Little House on the Prairie?*" Miss Augustine asked. She sat watching us eat.

"It's the only one I can find. I finished *Wrinkle in Time*. I even read it again. Mamalita takes me to the library every week but . . ." Yolanda squinted at me and I stopped.

"I'll ask your mother if I can take you by the library . . . I might even have some books 'round here from my girls. It just you two and your mother?"

Yolanda kicked my knee and pressed her finger against her lips so hard they blanched under her finger. "Her mother and my dad," I said.

"Oh." Miss Augustine put another spoon of green beans on my plate. "They at work a lot, huh?" She talked in a light, sort of slow voice like a teacher.

"All the time," I said. I stopped to finish chewing before I said, "The most we see of them is their dirty dishes. But I'm going to Mamalita's when Dad gets—"

"You are not going to no Mamalita, she don't want you and your mama don't want you neither!" Yolanda shouted at me. Miss Augustine grabbed her arm and shook her a little.

"Your grandmama?" she said to me.

"Yes, ma'am." I felt slack-mouthed full and set down my fork. I smiled at Miss Augustine so she'd know I really liked the food.

Miss Augustine took us around her townhouse to the garden she had in back, a rectangle of churned dirt full of tomato plants, collard greens, onion stalks going brown, basil plants growing all around the tomatoes, green and crookneck yellow squash vines, the squash longer than my hand. Miss Augustine asked Yolanda to pick the red tomatoes but Yolanda just stood there so Miss Augustine pushed her to her knees and stood over her until she started weeding. I got the tomatoes and cut the collards like Mamalita had shown me, down near the base so more would grow back. Miss Augustine said, "I'm getting you over here every week to help me," and patted my arm. I smelled Mamalita's house, fruit sugar and dust and lemon oil and biscuits. She snapped her fingers at Yolanda. "We going out in front and don't you try nothing. Get to weeding those beds."

The rose beds weeded and the spent heads cut off, Miss Augustine sent us to her upstairs bathroom to clean up and when we came down she had set the table again with bacon, lettuce and tomato sandwiches, more tea, and a spoon of green beans next to each sandwich. Yolanda at first wouldn't face the table and kept staring at the door, but by the time I'd finished half my sandwich, she was wolfing down her food, gobbling the sandwich in four bites and feeding the green beans onto her mouth one after the other until they were gone.

It was grayish outside, right before sundown. Miss Augustine held our hands and walked us back to our townhouse. She had us stand behind her. Philipa opened the door, Miss Augustine introduced herself and asked where the little girls were. "Upstairs," Philipa said. "I've been home a hour and not heard a peep."

Miss Augustine leaned back and folded her arms. "I have something for the bright one. Can you call her?"

"Bright smart or bright white?" Philipa said. My eyes burned and I wanted to jump out from behind Miss Augustine. Philipa yelled for us to come downstairs. Miss Augustine moved to stand behind us and when Philipa turned, her big smile went stiff and her eyes got icy-angry. She waddled over, her narrowed eyes looking at me, grabbed Yolanda's arm and yanked her into the house. I jumped in before she could touch me. "What are you doing coming in my house to take my children?"

"That one," Miss Augustine pointed at Yolanda, who hid all but her head behind Philipa and took on Philipa's mean look, "was sitting in a car with four men from who knows where. Front door wide open. No food in the Frigidaire." She talked to Philipa like she didn't notice her tight voice or hot look. Miss Augustine patted me on the head. "Anytime you need some help, send them over. I'm retired and my time is my own. I got gardening to do all the time. And I got two girls down at Tougaloo. Good babysitters. You knock on my door anytime," she said to me with a smile.

After Miss Augustine left, Philipa pushed us up the stairs to our room and watched while we put on pajamas. "The next time you leave this house, don't fucking come back," she said. She turned out the light and slammed the door.

"Don't come back?" I said.

"Shh. If she hears you, she'll whip us 'til tomorrow," Yolanda said, eyes wide.

Right before I fell asleep, I thought that if Philipa told Mama I'd left the house without permission, Mama would make me come back before I saw Mamalita. "Do you think she'll tell?" I said. Yolanda, eyes closed, folded her arms and turned her back to me.

· · ·

Dad had a Sunday off. He and Philipa slept late. Not even Mike was wandering around.

I'd made Yolanda some jelly sandwiches for breakfast. I had just a glass of milk, which now felt like Elmer's glue in my stomach. I was afraid to ask Philipa anymore if I could call my mother to see if she'd gotten a letter from Mamalita; when I had asked, she'd stared down at me so hard it felt like my blood dropped to my feet. Mamalita had me sit at the table every Sunday after church, still in my church clothes with ribbons in my hair, to write Mama a letter that she never answered but I knew that she got because when I got home, all the letters were there on Mama's dresser in a neat pile, opened so carefully they still looked stuck closed.

"What in the hell are you doing out here?" Philipa, her bra an enormous white band, her wide panties loose and grayish, filled the doorway. "Get your asses in here!"

We followed her to the bedroom and Philipa went into the drawers. I had picked out my own clothes since kindergarten, except for church; every Sunday Mama, or in summer Mamalita, laid an outfit on my bed while I ate breakfast. "Are we going to church?" I said.

Philipa selected matching outfits—nearly sheer embroidered white shirts and blue-and-red short shorts, the same size though I was taller and a little wider than Yolanda. The clothes reminded me of the woman down the street Mama and Mother Dear liked to talk about who had three little kids, no husband and more men friends than Mama. In summer, the woman had barbecues most Saturdays with a cheap round grill placed on the corner, her kids running around the block and into the street, and men with beer cans surrounding her, smiling, her too-short shorts revealing all her legs and her breasts almost pouring out of the halter top when she bent over the cooler for another beer. I could hear Mama rumbling in a low but still sharp-toned voice: slut, fast, loose, destined-for-trouble.

"I even have the ribbons to match," Philipa said. "Yolanda can wear the red ones, you look like Snow White in red."

I leaned toward the dresser and Philipa pulled me back so hard my legs tangled and I fell against Yolanda. "I want to wear . . . I don't want to wear the same thing as Yolanda."

Philipa slammed the door shut and the walls quivered.

"We gotta get dressed or Mama will get mad."

"She's already mad. She's always mad. She's no mama of mine. And where's camp, huh? We been staying home by ourselves all this time. I'm telling Dad—"

"No, don't!"

". . . and I'm going to Mamalita."

I put on jeans, a tee-shirt and my tennis shoes.

"Sandi!"

I got as far as the top step. Philipa blocked the way just standing there. "And where are you going?" Philipa said.

"Downstairs. To Dad."

"I told you to get—"

"I have to ask him some—"

Then I was on the floor, the side of my head hurt, all I could see was Philipa's fat face. "—interrupt when I'm talking!" I realized she had hit me. She leaned away. Dad stood behind her, hand on her shoulder. His other hand reached out to help me up, then we sat on the stairs. Philipa went into the bedroom to yell at Yolanda though Yolanda had stayed in the room and probably gotten dressed. "You need to listen to Phil, pie, while you're here."

"No."

He sighed. "Why not?"

"I can't . . . the clothes don't fit right." It felt like eyes were on me, like I'd be stripped and forced to walk through the middle of town but my hair would not grow to cover me up. Dad hugged me but it didn't help. He whispered the clothes were fine for one day, just do it once, for him, for Phil, and I wouldn't have to wear them again.

"Let's keep her happy, just today," he said. I knew I was going to do what he wanted, no matter how scared I was. I nodded. "That's my cream pie." He kissed me on the head, the only kiss I'd gotten since the first week. My eyes teared up with guilt.

• • •

We didn't go to church. We went to see a friend of Philipa's, in a different neighborhood, an older one, with lots of trees and wood houses. The front of the house had all kinds of bright flowers, a green birdbath, a circle of white brick as a front stoop. Inside, though, the curtains were closed, the blinds at the patio doors were closed, the walls were dark wood and even the carpet and much of the furniture was some kind of brown. I knew I was glowing in all that darkness. The shirt on Yolanda came to her waist but on me, it stopped just above my navel. I kept my arms folded over my stomach and needed another set of arms to fold over my butt; I could feel the shorts creeping higher, seams pressing into my skin.

"And this is Yetta," Philipa said. I thought she meant the woman but the woman smiled at me and said, "Yetta and Yolanda, how cute."

"They're almost the same age," Philipa said with a big smile. "But you can't get them mixed up, can you?"

My birthday was on the Epiphany and a year and a half before Yolanda's birthday. Dad must have forgotten my birthday to let her say that. And why did she call me Yetta? While they talked, Yolanda watched their faces and I studied the sculpted brown carpet, wondering how you could tell if something spilled or one of the cats in the house messed on it.

The woman slid open the patio door to let us into the yard. Rose bushes hugged the walls of the house. In back was a swing, but the tree it was tied to was too small to hold us.

"Bye!" Philipa said from the patio door.

Yolanda just waved. I ran to the glass door and saw Dad and Philipa at the front door with the woman and a man, shaking hands, saying goodbye. It closed. The inside was so dark I couldn't see anyone but I knew they were gone.

I was still looking through the glass door when the woman slid it open and came outside.

"Where'd they go?" I said.

"It's their honeymoon," she said. "They need some time alone."

"Why?"

She smiled at me and patted my shoulder. "Are you cold, hon?"

• • •

Yolanda called them Miss Alice and Mister Tom. Miss Alice worked with Philipa at the hospital. Yolanda had stayed with them from Good Friday, the day after her dad dropped her off with Philipa, until the week before they all came to get me in New Orleans.

Miss Alice served us big chunky chicken sandwiches for lunch, and pound cake for dessert. She looked buttery like the cake and smiled at me a lot. She didn't glow in the dark house so I thought I might not. I felt better after dinner and all her smiles.

Yolanda and I were playing cards by the patio door when Miss Alice told us she was going to work and would be back while we were asleep.

"Okay," Yolanda and I said.

I could see no clocks in the house but the sun was starting to go down. When it was totally dark Mister Tom brought us a snack—milk and raisins, a kindergartner snack—and turned the TV to a Godzilla movie. I ate only a few raisins.

"Drink your milk, Yetta," Mister Tom said.

"It's good," Yolanda said, "it tastes like vanilla." He smiled at her and looked at me with wide, waiting eyes.

I sipped. It tasted like melted vanilla ice cream. I drank it all down and gave Yolanda the rest of my raisins. Soon I felt sleepy—the movie I'd seen several times before, the dark brown walls and carpet, the TV the only light in the room. I curled up on the sofa.

• • •

I woke gagging, my body jerking, couldn't breathe my mouth was so full and the vomit was stuck in my throat with nowhere to go. I thought my eyes were open but all I saw was black. I tasted something salty and nasty-sour along with the milk vomit. I felt totally cold, like my thin clothes were gone, too.

Then Miss Alice was there, I could tell by the hand on my forehead. I was lifted. I could hear Miss Alice whispering to someone, a sheet snapped open, water sloshing in a container. The towel Miss Alice wiped on my face, neck and chest was warm and soft. "You'll be all right, hon." Slowly, through what seemed like mist, I saw Miss Alice's buttery face. She wrapped me in a puffy bathrobe. "Get some more rest, Yetta. You'll feel better in a little while." I tried to apologize for throwing up in her house. As I fell asleep I wondered where Miss Alice's children were and at how lucky they were.

"No, really . . . Better." Miss Alice's voice. I looked and she was on the phone. I felt weak and shaky, my mouth and throat still salty, dirty and so sour I could smell it. "I think . . . Oh, I . . . See you tomorrow."

She felt my forehead then sat on the bed. "Are you feeling any better?"

"My mouth is dirty."

She helped me to the bathroom. I rinsed my mouth and gargled, had juice, and went back to sleep.

We stayed the night. In the suitcase left for us sometime was another set of matching outfits—green short shorts with bright yellow tee-shirts that said on the front and back "Hot Stuff." No underwear. No toothbrushes. No hairbrush or comb. I sat on the bed, still in the robe, staring at the "Hot Stuff" on the shirt. As he passed the room, Mister Tom said it was a cute shirt. I thought he was naked. I was sure he'd been naked. And his thing dripping milk.

• • •

It was quiet on our townhouse block like no one lived there but Yolanda and me, like a Sunday with everyone at church.

We played hide and seek. I looked behind the townhouse for Yolanda but I didn't think she would hide in the tall grass and scratchy bushes. I peeked in the kitchenette window, in case she was running to a new hiding place inside, but saw just the stove and the skillet on the front burner, bacon grease turned white and solid. When I got to the front, Mike was in the open doorway, his head inside the house. He wore blue cut-off pants with some paint stains on them, some of the stray threads hanging as low as his ankles, a paint-smeared t-shirt, red tennis shoes and no socks, the outsides of his ankles gray with dust or dry skin.

"We're playing hide and seek," I said. He grunted. "Yolanda's in there somewhere."

"You seen them boys around?"

"No."

He put his hands in his pockets and jiggled change. "You want something from the store?"

"I want some Sugar Babies," Yolanda said, jumping out from behind the front door.

He glanced at her then faced me. "What you want?"

Yolanda crept up next to me so he would be looking at both of us. "A Jolly Rancher," I said.

"Watermelon?"

"Yeah," Yolanda said.

"Strawberry or green apple," I said.

He ran across the empty block, grass now so dry it was dark brown and flat, to the cluster of concrete buildings on the street running beside the highway, one of which was the store, we knew, because we'd seen kids with bottles and candy leaving the building. I thought another might be a laundromat since some days I could smell wet detergent though the townhouse had no laundry room, and probably none of the others did either.

Yolanda started jumping up and down, her grin so big it looked like two fingertips could fit in each cheek dimple.

"Wait 'til I tell Mama," she said.

"Tell her what?"

Yolanda pouted her lips. "Don't you know nothing? He likes you."

"No he doesn't."

"Uh-huh. He went to the store, didn't he?" And she smiled big and wide, like that answered everything.

Mike came back with two green apple Jolly Ranchers and a bag of Sugar Babies for Yolanda. We sat together on the small square of stoop, Mike in the middle, our hips touching his so we'd stay on the square. Over the sweet candy I could smell sweaty shoes and the musty smell of the sun on his T-shirt. He never wore socks and his clothes always looked cut off, faded, too big sometimes, and old. I wanted to ask where he lived because we never saw him leaving or going into one of the townhouses on the block; he would just be there, with or without the boys, sometimes with his baseball bat, sometimes just walking up and down the block, like he was looking for somebody.

"When your mom get back from work?" he said, facing front, not talking to either of us or to both, I wasn't sure. "She your mom? Or yours?"

"Ours," Yolanda said. "We're sisters."

He smiled for the first time. His face seemed to turn a lighter brown and he showed perfect white teeth in dark gums. "I can look and tell you not blood sisters," he said to me, still smiling.

Yolanda got on her knees and leaned toward him. "We're sisters now, that's what Mama says."

"It's my dad and her mom," I said. "I'm from New Orleans. I'm usually with Mamalita in the country." When I said that, I felt like pouting or hiding inside. "Where do you live?"

Mike stood up, stretched and groaned then poked his head into the townhouse. "Y'all got a radio?" He looked around and stepped inside, hands in his pockets. "What y'all had for breakfast?"

"Bacon and eggs and grits," Yolanda said, jumping to her feet to follow Mike inside. But Philipa had made all that for Dad and by the time we got our teeth brushed and clothes on, Dad was gone and the only food was the leftovers on their plates.

"No we didn't," I said, looking Yolanda in the eyes. She made a mean face back, squinting her eyes and wrinkling up her face and mouth.

As Mike walked through to the kitchenette and looked in the refrigerator, Yolanda hopped around the living room, kicking the *Little House* book and the Barbies under the sofa and chairs. I pushed her down in a chair and got my book back.

"Y'all got any money?" Mike said. "I could get something at the store."

Yolanda ran upstairs. Mike sat on the opposite end of the sofa. I opened the book.

"You read?" he said.

"Yeah."

"I mean, you like reading?"

"Yeah. Yolanda won't let me though."

"Probably can't read too good," Mike said. "My uncle's like that. He— "

Yolanda pounded down the stairs as fast as she could and dropped some dollar bills into Mike's hand. "Let me see the book cover," he said to me. I held it up. He nodded one more time and walked out without saying anything else. Yolanda skipped after him to the door and sat on the stoop to wait. Since she was quiet and not interested in me, I started reading.

• • •

I looked up from page twenty-five to Yolanda's shadow on the entryway floor, wisps of hair floating around her head like a halo, her shoulders rising and dropping with sighs. I hadn't helped her with her hair that morning—she could braid or twist it herself but needed me to comb and brush it into place, especially as her roots grew out thick and snarled. I felt tight in the throat like I did sometimes when I realized Mama would be home soon and I hadn't washed the breakfast dishes or gotten the mail from the mailbox. Then I swallowed and went back to my book. No one, not Philipa or Dad, would notice. When Dad was home, he was sleeping and we had to be quiet. I saw traces of him—plates, a dot of shaving cream in the bathroom sink, a smudged glass with a ring of juice at the bottom.

When the sun had dropped lower and started to orange, Yolanda was still waiting. Flies and mosquito hawks flew in around her. She slapped her arms—mosquitoes. She finally stood up and slammed the door closed as hard as she could. The pictures bounced on the wall and I crossed my fingers they wouldn't fall.

· · ·

Each morning by ten, Yolanda was in the open doorway, waiting for Mike and the boys to show up. She said they were better than television. I was bored with Barbies; all Yolanda knew or wanted to do was marry the Barbies to Ken, all of them, even though I said no one could do that for real, and have them cook pebbles and seeds and kiss him and lay down naked with him so I had put mine in the bottom of my suitcase and refused to get them out. After a couple days of giving Yolanda the confused, blank look she gave me when I mentioned libraries or books, she stopped asking. I had read the *Little House* book and *A Wrinkle in Time* three times each and felt like I could recite almost any page, just give me the number and the first word. I went with Yolanda to the door to wait, too. At least they were something to look at. TV was boring, soap operas or stations so fuzzy it wasn't worth trying to figure out what was going on.

Under the mailbox at the curb was a paper bag. Yolanda ran to get it, looked inside then, with a sour face, dropped it on the sidewalk, came back to sit and hung her head like she'd never been so disappointed. I looked in—books. And a note from Miss Augustine. She'd found the books in her daughters' room and I could keep them. She also said to drop by anytime for lunch or to help in the garden. I didn't even look at what they were, just brought them in, sat by the living room window and started reading the first one I took out of the bag—*Harriet Tubman, Conductor on the Underground Railroad.*

It took awhile to realize that I was not hearing birds high in trees, the whisper of running water, the soft step Ben said was like an Indian but the here and now, boys yelling and taunting. I felt dry-eyed and a little dizzy. Yolanda squealed then ran inside with something in one hand and raced up the stairs, taking two at a time and holding the rail so tight it swayed in and out as she grabbed and let go. And behind her was Mike. Upstairs she giggled, squealed once more then they were quiet. I went back to my book.

A car door slammed. My heart jumped because I had been holding my breath while John took his wife and child from the courthouse, a ruse to run away with them before they were sold, the three alone on the empty noontime street where anything could happen. I wanted to run upstairs to see if Mike was still in the townhouse with Yolanda, but I curled tighter into the corner by the window, partly hidden by the sofa, I hoped. I peeked out and my view of the street was blocked by Philipa's long green Pontiac. The front door opened. Philipa stomped from kitchenette to dining table to living room. She lit a cigarette. Yolanda giggled upstairs and I thought Philipa would go up to see what was going on but she acted like she didn't hear it and went back to the kitchenette.

Yolanda tiptoed down the stairs, looking around, Mike after her, putting on his T-shirt. She put her finger to her lips but Mike didn't try to walk lightly. He noticed me, nodded at me and went out the door. I finally took a deep breath; I felt unsteady and my ribcage hurt from holding my breath. Philipa walked out of the kitchenette with two sandwiches and Yolanda followed her to the table. Philipa looked at her twice, the second time a long time; I thought she'd yell at her about her hair being messed up or notice the bruise on her neck but all Philipa did was sit at the table to eat. And Yolanda looked over at me with a big baby smile.

Philipa said nothing about the bruise, if she even saw it. To me, Philipa had stayed in the kitchen just long enough for Mike to leave, like she knew he was there. I knew what Mama cared about—good grades, clean floors, made-up beds, chores on Saturday, church every Sunday—but Philipa lived in the townhouse like we weren't there.

That night I said, "What'd you do up here?" Yolanda looked at me, her eyes in the greenish light deep-set and bulging. "What'd you and Mike do up here?" She turned her face away but I saw a shadow in her cheek, a dimple. "What?"

She turned to me with a huge, green-tinted grin. "You gotta ask him."

• • •

In five days I read four of the books Miss Augustine gave me—*Mary McLeod Bethune, Frederick Douglass, Fahrenheit 451, Jane Eyre.* There were a dozen more books, including *Watership*

Down, *The Three Musketeers*, *The Count of Monte Cristo*, a book of Bradbury short stories I'd read before, and a couple of adult novels by the woman who wrote the *Harriet Tubman* book. I carried the bag from bedroom to living room to stoop to dining table; when Yolanda started sighing as loud as she could I went into the downstairs closet.

• • •

Philipa told us to do laundry by kicking Yolanda's clothes out of the corner, dumping both my suitcases, even clothes that were clean, and dragging in two hampers, towels from the bathroom and their clothes.

"We can't do laundry without money," I said.

She threw a ten-dollar bill at me but it fluttered to the carpet. I laughed. She stomped to her bedroom and slammed the door. Yolanda went downstairs for the two grocery carts she used for laundry. She said right after she came to the townhouse from Miss Alice's, Philipa dumped the laundry in her room and told her to go do it but Dad came later to the laundromat to help her finish. She said it evenly, like she was telling me how old she was.

"It's so great to have a sister," Yolanda said as we wheeled the carts down the middle of the street. "It's hard to pull two at the same time."

It was early afternoon so the laundromat, which was right where I'd smelled it, was empty. We filled a row of washers, then went to the little store next door for detergent and candy. The store was cramped; the aisles weren't big enough to walk side by side so I followed Yolanda through and she went up and down every aisle, dust on the jars of mustard and pickles and boxes of macaroni and cheese, every shelf full like no one ever shopped there. We found a small box of detergent, just enough,

Yolanda said. We got Jolly Ranchers, too—watermelon for
Yolanda, green apple for me and on our way out, I saw a pay
phone.

I thought about it while I crunched the Jolly Rancher. I had
wondered why Mama hadn't called, why Mamalita hadn't called,
why I hadn't just picked up the phone and called home. But
nothing except what was in my suitcase felt like mine. Even
Dad didn't feel like mine anymore and when I thought of him,
what came to mind was his graduation picture, his Afro like fur
trim on the dark blue mortar and board, his closed-mouth smile,
not what he looked like now. After the clothes were in dryers, a
row of twirling red, yellow, orange, blue and black and two dryers just swirls of white, I went back to the pay phone, Yolanda
following.

"Who are you calling? A boy?" she said with a big, dimpled
smile.

"Mama."

"She's at home."

"That's your mama, not mine."

Her smile dropped away. "You can't do that."

"Are you going to tell?"

"Mama said you can't call home. Nobody wants you there."

"Oh, shut up. Go watch the clothes. *Go.*" She slipped away.

Once Mama realized it was really me, she said, "I've been
worried. Have you seen Mamalita? Where are you?"

"Meridian."

"Where? With who?"

"Dad. Yolanda. Philipa."

I heard rustling and other voices, men's voices. "What's the
phone number?"

"I don't know."

"Shit, you been there how long and didn't have sense enough

to learn the phone number?" I heard laughing. "All right then, what's the address? You know that at least, don't you?" More laughing. She made me promise to call with the phone number by Sunday though she didn't have to make me promise. Even hearing her mad made me homesick. I suddenly felt like I had to get back to Mama or else. I felt how mad and scared I'd been, how much I hated Yolanda following me around, how much I hated seeing Dad so little I'd almost forgotten what he looked like. I was glad of one thing—my own clothes, clothes that covered my belly and butt at the same time, would be clean soon.

"Should we fold them?" I said.

"We can do it later."

She seemed quiet. I knew she would tell. "Do you want to call your dad?"

She jumped like she'd been hit. "I-I don't know the number, not anymore."

"When you find it, we can call him."

"Mama says if he wanted me he wouldn't've left me here . . ."

Right then she seemed much lonelier than me and I swore to God I'd help her. We pulled the carts back to the townhouse in silence. Dad's Fiat was there. It was late afternoon and he had never been home that early. I rang the doorbell and he looked surprised to see me on the other side of the door.

"So there you are," he said. He pulled the carts in for us. Philipa came downstairs and smiled big at us like she hadn't forced us out the house. Dad started to fold the laundry with us and Philipa helped. Yolanda whispered later that Philipa had never helped before, not even hanging clothes; she made Yolanda carry a chair upstairs.

Yolanda helped Philipa with the dishes. I tiptoed upstairs to Dad and knocked on the doorjamb of the bedroom because I didn't see him. He came to the door, beer in one hand, cigarette in the other.

"Hey, cream pie. What's happening?"

"Dad, when can I see Mamalita?"

"Soon. I just need more than one day off in a row."

"We haven't been going to camp."

"Oh, out this week?" I followed him to the bathroom where he put down the beer and lathered his face to shave.

"No, we haven't been at all. We're here in the house all day."

He stopped for a few seconds then rubbed his face faster. "Oh." He rinsed his hand and looked at me in the mirror. "Did you two offer to do laundry or Phil tell you to?"

"She just dumped all the clothes out and threw money at us." I stopped, not wanting to tell him about Mike upstairs or Miss Augustine bringing Yolanda and me back to the town-house. Dad stared at me and I looked down.

"I'll take care of it."

I smiled. I knew he would. After Yolanda and I brought our clothes upstairs, I put all my neatly folded clothes in my suitcase, sure I'd be at Mamalita's soon.

Their voices woke me that night, Dad and Philipa through doors, Dad's voice sounding deep and angry and Philipa's rapid and high. I poked Yolanda with my elbow and she jumped up. When she heard them, she curled up under the covers. Then they were quiet. I moved slow and quiet to their door. No sounds. Then some moans and whispers. Asleep, I guessed. I tiptoed downstairs since even Yolanda or I could make the staircase vibrate. On the table in the dining patch was the telephone bill. I found a pen and copied the phone number, address, and even zip code on the inside of my arm.

• • •

I woke to rumbles and tiny wet slaps, the first rain all summer. I didn't get up to look at Dad's and Philipa's door, just guessed they were not there. I had dreamed Mister Tom crawled into the bedroom, put his thing into my mouth and poked my tongue and teeth and the back of my mouth until I threw up. The cramps still in my stomach told me it wasn't just a dream, that he was why I threw up. While I was watching rain smear pinkish dirt on the window, Yolanda woke up, gasped and bounced off the bed. "Rain?" she said. "Oh, great, no boys, no TV, and all you do is read stupid books—"

"You're stupid because you can't read."

"I can too."

I snatched up the book I had been reading, *The Count of Monte Cristo*, and held it out to her. She looked at it like a snake then up at my face to see if I was serious. She got dressed right away, another of the short, tight matching outfits Philipa had bought us—shorts with wide red, blue, green and white stripes, an almost sheer light blue shirt with no sleeves and a deep V in front.

Yolanda stuck her nose up in the air when I came downstairs in my cutoffs and a t-shirt, the bag of books under my arm; the paper was getting worn and soft and had small tears in the bottom corners. She had made her own breakfast—two slices of dark toast with grape jelly thick on top. I had cereal. Then she did something she never did—after lunch I usually washed the dishes from Philipa's and Dad's breakfast but this time, Yolanda filled the sink with hot water and squirted in soap. She looked at me over her shoulder a few times until I turned my back to her.

"Yolanda? Mister Tom ever . . . do something to you?"

"We played cards one time."

"Not like that, I mean did he ever take his pants off?"

"Uh-huh."

"Did he put something in your mouth? After he took his pants off?"

"You mean touch his thing? They like that."

I turned to look at her because she answered so evenly, like we were talking about crayon colors. "Has he done it to you before?"

"I can't tell, it's a secret."

"Whose secret?"

Her hands in the soapy water stopped moving and she screwed up her face, confused. "Mine?"

"You're seven, Yolanda, don't you—"

"I'm eight."

"You're eight in August and this is July—"

"I'm almost—"

"No almost, you are seven and I am nine and he shouldn't be putting—"

I heard a tinkle and she said, "Oh no!" She held up a glass, the top half broken off. I went over, stuck a finger in the almost-boiling hot dishwater then in the water running from the faucet.

"It broke 'cause the dishwater is too hot and the rinse water is all cold."

"It's your fault. You're supposed to do the dishes." She held the broken glass out to me.

"Nobody told me I have to do anything. You started 'em, you finish 'em."

I opened the front door to see the rain. I expected dark clouds but saw only one that was gray, the rest lighter, the sun streaming through clouds on the empty block across the street. Near the highway, some boys huddled under the side awning near the store, one bouncing a tennis ball. The rain was light; I held out my arm and the drops were so warm they felt soft and barely wet. The patch of sun grew until it filled the empty block and crossed the street, making the grass in front of the townhouses shine. One of the boys held his arm out, felt no rain and went back into the store. I squinted and shielded my eyes but none of the boys left was tall enough to be Mike. Then he came up our block, swinging his baseball bat, looking at the ground. He was in the same clothes I'd first seen him in, clothes he wore most times we saw him. I sat on the stoop near the doorway, where it was dry. Like in New Orleans, the hot sun started evaporating the water on the street and sidewalks, a vapor rising up from the asphalt, wet heat rising even from the dry concrete I sat on.

"Hey!" Yolanda screamed above me. Mike stopped swinging his bat and walked over to us.

"Y'all seen them boys? he said.

"You want a cold drink?" Yolanda said.

"I saw some by the store," I said without lifting my head. I looked at the book though I couldn't concentrate with Mike standing there.

"She ain't seen nothing, all she do is read," Yolanda said.

Mike sat down next to my bag and looked inside. Yolanda snorted behind me. I first thought he'd look through, grunt and go inside with Yolanda again, but he picked out each one, looked at the front and back covers, and carefully stacked them back in the bag. I heard a car but paid no attention—if it was Philipa, Yolanda would run inside and I'd follow; if it was anyone else, they wouldn't pass us here at the end of the block. Then I heard my name.

Miss Augustine stood by her green and white Pinto, a bag of groceries in one arm, her other arm waving me over. I looked up at Yolanda; she had turned her back to Miss Augustine, her lips pouted out as far as they could.

"Who that?" Mike said.

"Miss Augustine," I said. "She gave me the books."

"Which ones you read? You read this one?" He held up the Bradbury stories.

"I like the one about the house with no people," I said as I got up to see Miss Augustine. The sidewalk wasn't completely dry yet and getting hotter against my bare feet. Yolanda had sat down next to Mike but he had the Bradbury book open close to his face.

"How you doing there, Sandrine?" Miss Augustine shifted the bag to her other arm and unlocked her door, cool air rushing at my damp toes.

"Thank you for the books."

"My pleasure." She glanced over at our townhouse before going inside. I followed. "That girl reading any?"

"No. Ma'am," I added though Miss Augustine didn't look sideways at me. "I still have to go in the closet sometimes."

Miss Augustine smiled a little. "I was gonna make me some teacakes before it got too hot. You girls want to help?"

"Yolanda won't come."

Miss Augustine took butter out of the refrigerator. "Then we won't miss her," she said with a sweet smile. She watched me wash my hands at the sink but didn't say anything until I was seated on the floor, ceramic bowl between my knees, stirring and smashing the sugar into the butter, the way Mamalita and I did, taking turns, blending it well so the teacakes would brown evenly and taste gently sweet.

Miss Augustine bent down and touched my arm. "Sandrine, what's that on your arm?"

My chest filled with something other than air and my eyes burned. I wanted to tell Miss Augustine everything, Yolanda and Philipa at K & B, Mike and Yolanda, the matching clothes, Mr. Tom, Philipa hitting me. "My mother wants the phone number so I wrote it down," I said.

Miss Augustine took the bowl and stirred but too slowly to mix it right. Her gray eyes on me were kind and comforting but I could tell behind her eyes a lot of thinking was going on and that scared me. "She doesn't have it now?" I couldn't talk so I shook my head. "Does she have the address?" she said.

"I called her. From the pay phone." I waved at the door, sort of toward the store and laundromat.

"So she didn't know where you were?"

"I guess not. I guess Mamalita doesn't either. Dad said he'd bring me when he had enough time off but he's always . . ."

Suddenly Miss Augustine jumped to her feet. "Let's get these teacakes ready and then you can call her from right here." She looked at my face then smiled. "I won't tell nobody. Our secret. You can come here anytime to call your mama, hear?"

"Yes, ma'am."

When the teacakes were in the oven, I called Mama from Miss Augustine's kitchenette while Miss Augustine heated up some lunch for me. I had expected Mama to be proud I'd called back, or happy but she asked for the phone number right after saying hello, then asked where Dad worked, where Philipa worked, what Yolanda and I did all day, when Dad was home from work. All I could tell her was he was off usually one day a week. Miss Augustine traded me the phone for a plate piled with macaroni, greens and ham slices. I was so hungry I sighed when I swallowed. When I was done, Miss Augustine, the phone still to her ear, wrapped three teacakes in a paper towel and told me to go on back before I was missed and she'd see me later, maybe that night.

The sun was hot and the slice of shade on the front stoop, and Mike, were gone. At Mamalita's we spent the heat of the day on the porch. After lunch and a second load of laundry, the first load on the line dry as paper, or a walk to the store a few blocks away for a Coke and a popsicle, or starting ice cream on Sunday, the trees in front of the house shaded the porch and the concrete cooled enough to sit on. But on this block there were no trees along the street, like they had all been mowed down, the only ones left in the dead end jungle where they cast an inch of shade that by dinner was two inches; if you tried to shelter in it from the sun, your toes would burn.

Mike was sprawled across the sofa, the Bradbury book still close to his face. I looked around for the bag to get the Dumas book. I looked in the closet, in the kitchen cabinets, even the refrigerator. Mike made a loud, long yawn.

"What you looking for?" he said.

"The books."

He pointed at the ceiling. The toilet flushed and water bubbled and rushed through the pipes in the wall. I went up the first few stairs then doubled back and stood next to him until he looked around the side of the book at me. He didn't look fourteen, he looked older.

"Where do you live?" I said. He just blinked and shifted his eyes back to the book. "Do you live around here? What'd you do to Yolanda that other day?" His eyebrows went up but he didn't stop looking at the book. The toilet flushed again but sounded muffled. I'd get to Yolanda later. "How she get that bruise on her neck?"

He closed the book on his finger, swung his long legs over and sat up straight, studying me, looking hard at my face then up and down me. I backed away a little. "How old are you?" he said.

"Eight."

He snorted. "You let me read this? I bring it back tomorrow."

With the third flush, no water coursed through the pipes in the wall and I heard Yolanda squeal. When I got to the second floor landing, I saw the beige carpet in the hall outside the bathroom slowly turning dark. Yolanda stood by the toilet stabbing the stick of the plunger in the toilet. The water on the floor was deep enough to cover my little toes and light brown pieces floated in it. I saw in the corner the bag of books, the bottom completely wet. And then I saw what was clogging the toilet—book pages torn and stopping up the bowl. Breathing fast, water on the floor ice cold around my feet, I wanted to hit her but instead I snatched the plunger out of her hand, grabbed her arm and pushed her out of the bathroom so hard she hit the wall across from the bathroom and almost fell down. I wanted to apologize but instead gave her a mean look and slammed the door closed. There was so much water the towels I spread out turned dark right away and water pooled on top. The hole in the toilet bowl was packed with wet paper, the words melting stripes, a dent in the middle where Yolanda had tried to force it down. It was an almost solid mass so I pulled most of it out and, gagging, stuck my hand a little down the hole to get any pages stuck in there. It was clear and clean so I flushed down the tiny floating pieces. In the bag the book on top, *Watership Down*, a few hundred pages thick, was wet from the middle to end. The other books left were all dark and stuck together. She'd only torn up two books—*Jane Eyre* and *The Count of Monte Cristo*.

The door opened and Yolanda stood there, an almost-smile on her face. Then I heard the pounding. I thought Mike was running upstairs but then Philipa splashed into the doorway. I held up the wad of wet paper, ready to explain. Philipa slapped it out of my hand, grabbed my wrists and half-dragged me out of the bathroom. I wanted to scream for Dad but before I could, my back hit the bedroom door, it opened and I was on the floor. "She broke the glass, too, Mama." I heard Yolanda but couldn't see her around Philipa, whose huge breasts were heaving up and down, her hands on her hips, her eyes now narrow and mean.

"Get back in that room, you little whore!" Philipa said over her shoulder. She slapped the wet bag of books into my chest. "Take them back," she said to me.

"I can't." Philipa hit me on the top of the head with the flat of her hand. I tasted metal like I'd chewed pennies. "Ow." She hit me again, harder this time, hard enough for me to feel the bands of her rings in my scalp.

"You can take them back or I can beat your damn head off. Who do you think you are, talking back to me? Who do you think is taking care of you? Do you see your father here, do you? No." She pushed me at the stairs and I caught the rail just as my feet slid over the first two steps. I was glad Mike was gone when I got downstairs.

I had to hold the bag and books wrapped in my arms. I felt every pock in the concrete, every weed and pebble as I passed the teal and green townhouses to Miss Augustine's. I looked over at the townhouse; I could stand at Miss Augustine's stoop a minute or two then hide the books in my suitcase but Philipa stood on the stoop, hands still on her hips.

I rang the bell, my throat tight, my head stuffed full. When the door opened, I just held the wet bag up to her. I couldn't look in her face. She'd given me the books and now I was giving them back dripping wet and ruined, books I hadn't even read yet, and she'd been so nice to me, I felt like I was spitting on her. My arms ached holding them up. When the weight lifted and I knew she'd taken them, I turned and walked away, tears itching my chin, my feet heavy. I'd never see Miss Augustine again. She might forgive me but I could never forgive myself. I felt betrayed and the guilt of betrayal.

When I opened the front door, Philipa grabbed my arm and dragged me up to Yolanda's room. Yolanda knelt by the bed.

"Kneel!" she said. I did. She leaned close to my ear but didn't whisper. "And pray to God to forgive you!" She stomped down the stairs then all the floors and walls shook as she ran back up the stairs. I saw the plates right before they crashed through the window. "They're still dirty." She slammed the door closed.

Tears slid down my cheeks until I was crying hard. We heard her pounding around the hall and her bedroom. We heard her talking loud on the phone and Yolanda swore she heard Philipa use our names. I cried harder, wanting Mama or Mamalita or Miss Augustine or Miss Alice or anybody, to be anywhere. Yolanda kneeled next to me praying, "And please, God, help my sister calm down because she's really upset." I couldn't believe Yolanda was so quiet about it, no tears, not even a sigh.

Through the jagged hole in the window I watched the sky turn orange then slowly darken, the air getting cooler and wetter. We had no idea why we were there, still kneeling hours later because Philipa hadn't told us we could move. No bathroom break. My bladder was full but my lips were dry and peeling. I put my forehead on the edge of the bed.

• • •

It was dark. I heard Dad's Fiat sputter into the driveway.

"I hate your mother," I said to Yolanda.

Yolanda cut her eyes at me then prayed harder, her head on her hands and her eyes squeezed shut, as if that would get her prayers to God faster.

"If God cared," I heard myself say, "He would've done something before."

"They're punished," Philipa said outside our door. We couldn't hear the rest of what she said.

I leaned close to Yolanda. "You think she—"

"That's enough, Phil," Dad said firmly. He opened the door,

peeked in and closed it. "I've never known Sandrine to lie or steal or break things."

"When are you here to know anything? You know she told that bitch down the street I don't buy food? You know she fucked up the toilet trying to flush books?"

The phone rang. And I started to pray. First I prayed it was Mama. Then I prayed it wasn't because if I had spent how long on my knees for unclogging the toilet and humiliating myself, what would he let her do to me for calling Mama? Or, and my empty stomach turned, what Miss Augustine told Mama.

We smelled dinner cooking.

We heard dishes washed.

We waited.

"My stomach hurts," Yolanda said.

"Mine too."

The door opened behind us. I jumped up from my knees, the pattern of carpet naps dented into my skin buckling. Dad waved his hands like he wanted us to be still. "Get ready for bed. We'll talk about it in the morning."

No, we won't, I thought.

I pretended to go to sleep right away. After Yolanda fell asleep, I sat up, the cool breeze coming in the broken window keeping me awake until Dad and Philipa's room was quiet.

I tiptoed to the bathroom for my toothbrush. My big suitcase was too heavy with everything in it so I put as much into the little one as I could, leaving my Barbies, dresses and white sandals. I fished out the twenty-dollar bill Mama hid in the lining of the big suitcase for emergencies. I wrote Yolanda a note, telling her goodbye and to call her dad if she wanted to get away, no one could stop her, though I knew Philipa could and would.

The street was quiet and damp. I followed the highway, past the closed corner store and laundromat that smelled like soap and lint even then. When the sidewalk ran out, I walked on the gravel shoulder. The street narrowed, the streetlights got further and further apart, the highway curved away and disappeared. In the dark I was afraid someone might sneak up on me but under streetlights I was afraid someone might find me and send me back to Dad and Philipa and Yolanda. The sidewalk started again when I reached big brick buildings, warehouses like near the river in New Orleans. As the sun started to color the sky I reached office buildings, squat closed stores with typewriters, dresses and candies in the windows. I smelled fried eggs and ham and my mouth filled with saliva. The smells got stronger and stronger, disappeared for half a block, and suddenly were there again stronger, and I saw light on the sidewalk from a diner. Inside men, black men, ate eggs and ham and biscuits and coffee before work. I thought about spending some of my twenty dollars on just eggs and juice, I was really hungry, but I had to get home before—

"Hey honey, what you doing out so early?" I heard behind me. I didn't recognize the voice but it was male, deep, Mississippian, definitely white. I turned. Police car, two white officers. The one leaning out the window looked older, a little wrinkled, and plump like a Santa Claus. I knew I couldn't outrun the car.

"I'm looking for the bus station," I said.

"That's right up the street there but, uh . . ." The Santa Claus officer looked past me into the diner. "Your daddy in there?"

I could tell by his tone he didn't think any of the black men in there could be my father. Some white people weren't sure what I was because of my skin, though I could never see how my wide flat nose or my big lips looked white. I felt evil, like when an old saleslady in Goudchaux's, hair gray like dirty soap, bent down and asked four-year-old me, ignoring Mama, if my maid would be paying for my dress; Mama had snatched up my arm and dragged me out of the store, spitting that we would go naked before we went in that or any Canal Street department store again and she held my arm so tight and pulled so hard all day I had bruises on my forearm the shape of her fingers. "No." Santa cop waited. I looked down at the sidewalk then thought of, "They left and I don't know where they're gone so I need to go back home to my mother." I talked as well as I could; if they thought I was white or weren't sure, they might let me walk on to the station and forget me.

"What she say?" the driver said. The big cop leaned in to tell then he reached behind him to open the back door. "Let's go see can't we find 'em, all right?" I didn't move. He laughed. "Don't be scared, sugar. We the police. This is our job. C'mon now. We can't leave you out here," he flicked his eyes at the diner windows and I tried not to get a hard look on my face, "by yourself."

I got in. I could tell them about Miss Alice but not only would Mister Tom be there, she would call Dad and Philipa but even worse, they would realize I was not white and might think I was a runaway, or trouble or just lose all concern and leave me anywhere. I wished I could face Miss Augustine but if I could've, I would have gone to her first. Then I remembered the empty townhouse at the end of the block. I told them the street and pretended to not remember the address. The big cop sat sideways so he could talk to me. I made up a name, said I'd come to visit my father but he and his new family moved suddenly and told me to go to the bus station and back home. I was surprised when he shook his head and said, "The things people do."

The sun was up when we reached the street and I slumped down so Dad or Philipa leaving early for work or Miss Augustine watering her roses wouldn't see me. The driver cop knocked on the door of the pale-green-trimmed townhouse, looked in the windows, walked around back. I peeked once out the side window and saw both Dad's Fiat and Philipa's green Pontiac in the driveway at the far end of the block.

The driver cop got back in. "Well," he said. "She's right. Nobody there. Look like they just moved out, too. Guess they didn't like the neighborhood," he said, smiling.

As we drove away, Santa cop chewed the inside of his mouth. "I guess we best take her to the Greyhound, huh? You got some money?" he said to me.

"Twenty dollars."

He rocked back and forth as the car passed over bumps and turned back toward the downtown area. He smiled. "How could they leave a cutie like you, huh?" I smiled back to be nice but his compliment made me sick.

He had been right—the Greyhound station was a block away from the diner. Both went inside with me. It was as bright inside as the diner had looked, wide streaks of dirt on the floor but when we passed the bathrooms, they smelled like candy-sweet pink soap. Rows of molded plastic chairs, pale turquoise, glowing orange and a green like pond scum, filled the middle of the floor, but the ticket counter looked out of an old Western, carved heavy wood and thick steel bars. After I bought my ticket, the cops brought me to the diner and got me some breakfast to go—eggs, biscuit, a slice of ham and a carton of milk—and I kept my eyes down so the men still eating wouldn't see me, wouldn't say "How you?" or nod; the cops would change, pinch their faces tight and, thinking me a liar or, worse, trying to pass, I might disappear and never be found. They brought me back and didn't leave until I was sitting down near the ticket counter eating. As soon as they were gone, I threw the milk away. I chewed everything forty times because my stomach had been empty since Miss Augustine's lunch and I didn't want to throw up anything.

Until the bus got on the highway, I was sure Dad or Philipa

or those two cops or Mister Tom and Miss Alice would come to the station or even stop the bus to get me off. I was so relieved when the driver sped up, I fell asleep.

• • •

I woke confused by the window on my right instead of left, the heavy plaid curtains and the closet door across from the foot of the bed. The air smelled like pepper, garlic and onions and I heard water running, cabinets closing, a chair pulled across the floor and women's voices. I lifted the plaid curtain with one finger, saw the wall and blacked out window next door and couldn't stop my smile. Slowly, I felt the softness of my own bed and the space around me, recognized the faded pink wallpaper and the bare hint of green leaves and white flowers that used to be there, and breathed in the smell of actual cooking. Then my heart jumped—I thought I'd slept all day and was smelling dinner. I heard Mama's voice, then Mother Dear's answering. I sat up and put my ear to the wall.

"All the help I need is sleeping in the bed like she got some maid to clean up that living room. Shit, rich people sleep, poor people *work*. And women with children missing do not have parties."

"It wasn't a party, Dear," Mama said tightly, "just some—"

"Like the welfare slut down the block has friends? You 'bout to get yourself knocked up and left on your ass again?"

Then my door flung open, the doorknob cracked into the wall and Mama stood in the doorway, hands on her hips, a long metal straining spoon sticking out of one fist like an extension of her arm. "Get up."

"I am up."

"Get in this kitchen now!" she said like I'd curled under the sheet or said the last thing I would ever do was help her. Dear stood behind Mama, arms folded, half her mouth and both eyes smiling as Mama stomped away from the door muttering and shaking her head. Dear always seemed happier when Mama had just yelled at me or I was doing chores. It probably galled her I'd been back almost twenty-four hours and she hadn't seen me clean, wash, cut, stack or dust anything.

I snatched a t-shirt and pair of cut-offs from the suitcase still open on the floor and hurried into them, zipping and snapping my shorts in the hall. When I realized which shirt it was I was already in the kitchen—Hot Stuff. I turned to go change when Dear said, "And where you going?"

Mama scowled over her shoulder and I thought she'd say something about the t-shirt but instead she pointed at Dear who, with a full smile that didn't seem at all happy, gave me the knife in her hand and left me the potatoes to cut into the huge soup pot heating on the stove. I stood on a stool to be high enough to drop in the chunks of potato without getting stung with almost-boiling water. Mama and Dear huddled over the sink, cutting up chicken and fish, Dear talking non-stop and Mama sighing, pursing her lips, once in awhile holding her eyes shut but saying little. As soon as I finished the potatoes, I set another big pot of water on to boil for macaroni, grated two pounds of cheese, and cut up onions and pickles. It felt like Thanksgiving with different food and when I opened my mouth to ask whose birthday it was or if we were selling plates like the lady across the street did Friday nights, Dear or Mama would hand me something to wash, peel, stir or chop. I didn't get to brush my teeth until folks started showing up, hugging Mama and Dear and patting me on the head. In the bathroom mirror I looked flushed in the cheeks and pale everywhere else, my hair frizzy on top but stuck to the sides of my face and neck. I knew if I went out looking like that Mama or Dear would pinch me by the shoulder or grab the back of my head and hiss in my ear about looking so trifling. I worked fast, brushing teeth with one hand and yanking out knots in my hair with the other.

By two o'clock there were people everywhere—an uncle and male neighbors on the front steps and porch, drinking cans of beer and talking loud, folks in the living room and hall, some kids bouncing on my bed, women filling the kitchen with the radio and their voices and heat from the stove and moving around each other to fill the table with food, people and kids even in the little square of yard we had. Mama's little sister, Auntie Z, was in from Baton Rouge and as I tried to squeeze past her, she grabbed the back of my neck and pressed me against her so hard I breathed the cotton of her t-shirt into my nose. "Oooh, little girl, I am so glad you're home," she said. She leaned me away and smiled big down into my face. "We thought we'd never see you again."

In the yard, Uncle Frank stood over the barbecue grill, so sweaty even his close-cropped hair dripped. The yard filled up behind me with people coming to get barbecued chicken to pile on plastic plates with squares of baked macaroni, lumps of potato salad, fried fish and slices of bread. Hands clapped on my shoulders, and I got my cheeks pinched a few times, but by the time I turned to see who, it was a confusion of dresses, shirts and bare arms in all shades of dark brown. There was no room to do anything but sit with the other kids eating. I felt like I'd been hungry for weeks and filled my plate three times, Mama smiling at me over and between heads each time.

By dusk, half the adults had gone but the ones still there looked like they'd settled in—Uncle Frank and Uncle Jerry were in front of the TV in the living room with some of Mama's friends yelling at wrestling and drinking more beer. The few parties I got to be around, at Christmas, on Mother's Day, at Easter, always ended with a few of Mama's friends still around, the TV on, her friends looking at each other waiting for the others to leave and usually I fell asleep before it was decided and only found out in the morning who stayed by seeing which car was left on the block or by studying the back walking out the door and down the stairs. I hadn't seen Joe Henry since people started coming though I had seen Raheem, the one who always told me to watch out for the indoctrination of the white man, to stop reading what they assigned in school and especially stop watching TV though Mama rarely let me and I didn't turn it on when she was gone; she usually felt the top of the console to make sure it was cold. Raheem was in there, too, watching white men wrestle in an auditorium in Tennessee or Kentucky somewhere.

The chairs brought from Dear's house were still scattered around the kitchen. Dear and Mama sat at the table, Mama picking at some fish, while Auntie Z and Aunt Margie washed the huge pots and Mama's friend Cherry divided up the food left onto twelve plates and wrapped them in foil. Mama waved me over to her.

"There she is," Auntie Z said, "the guest of honor." I looked at Mama and Auntie Z laughed. "You, girl! You the one that was missing, not Shirl."

"Worrying her mama to death," Dear said, not looking at me.

"Dear," Aunt Margie said quietly.

"What?" Dear snapped back.

Auntie Z raised her eyebrows and turned back to the sink.

Mama patted my arm and sighed. "Dear," she said slowly, "it's just you said that like it was her fault . . ."

"It's both y'all's fault," Dear said, baring her teeth. Auntie Z, Aunt Margie and Cherry all turned around and talked at once. Dear sat up straighter and talked over them. "You never should've trusted that man. You know he thinks—"

"We know what you think, Dear," Mama said.

"You," Dear pointed at Mama but glared at me, "were never no more than a damn slut anyway and got what you deserve."

Auntie Z put her arm around my shoulders. "And how long you been married, Dear?" Dear heaved forward to grab at Auntie Z but she was just out of reach. "Ain't a woman in this room been married even once and you, Dear, had six children with six—"

"No, it's five," Aunt Margie said as she stacked two foil-wrapped plates, " 'cause Frank and Tamira have the same—"

"No, that's Frank and Shirl got the same daddy," Auntie Z jumped in.

"No better than the so-called slut y'all like to talk about . . ." Cherry started.

"That woman barely knows the names of her children, much less the fathers," Mama said back, face as pulled down and wrinkled up as Dear's. A little smile curved onto Dear's mean face and even Mama sat up straighter. Aunt Margie walked out past me, muttering, ". . . bunch of damn wolves . . ." All the faces in the kitchen were twisted up, lips pursed or poked out, hands on hips, heads turned deliberately away from each other.

Two big yells came from the living room.

Auntie Z gave my shoulder a squeeze and whispered in my ear, "Go get some fresh air, all right?" She patted my back.

Uncle Jerry stood at the door, keys in hand, looking from Uncle Frank to Joe Henry, Raheem and another friend of Mama's, whose name I never remembered hearing, sitting in chairs by Mama's bed. Uncle Jerry's worried face broke into a huge grin when he saw me, and he opened the screen door for me to step out under his arm.

I went out to the porch. All the kids were gone. I only had two cousins, both younger and their mothers had taken them home, leaving Uncle Frank and Uncle Jerry; the other kids had wandered in from the neighborhood or come with Mama's friends. I sat on the steps. Three kids from down the block watched me from the sidewalk. Mama and Dear forbid me to play with these kids; Dear called their house on the corner a roach trap and Mama complained because they didn't always wear shoes and there were "too many" of them for one mother and no husband and Mama and Dear, anytime the mother put her grill and Styrofoam cooler out on the corner, camped out on our porch or Dear's all day muttering "trash . . . stupid . . . whorish," smiling and laughing out the meanest words in loud don't-care-who-hears voices. The oldest one, a girl a little younger than me, stepped closer. She looked at the lit up screen door then at me.

"Y'all had a party?"

"Sort of," I said.

"You back early."

I watched them through windows but I never thought they noticed anything about me. "Yeah," I said.

The men's voices got louder, not cheering or yelling at the TV but all talking. Chairs slid on the floor, a bottle rolled into the door and I heard Uncle Frank yell above all the rest, "If I'm going, all y'all niggers going, like I'm-a leave you here with . . ."

"Y'all go home," Dear yelled from the screen door. "And you get your ass inside."

I gave them a little smile and went in. I was glad to; I was tired from eating, squeezing through people, getting up early. Dear gave me a pinch when I passed her but I didn't complain, just ducked my way under waving men's arms and between Mama's and Auntie Z's hips straight to my room and lay on my bed. I didn't realize I'd fallen asleep until I woke the next morning.

• • •

Coughing woke me. Mama's voice through the wall sounded light and teasing—a friend had stayed over later than usual; they were usually gone by dawn for work or before Dear woke up and started peeking over to see what Mama was doing. Heavy flat footsteps made their way to the bathroom and I smelled coffee, something Mama kept for friends or relatives and never drank herself. I liked cleaning the percolator afterwards and scooping out the warm soft coffee grounds, another smell from Mamalita's house, and if there were a few spoonfuls of coffee left, I'd make myself coffee the way Mamalita made it for me Sunday mornings before church—a glass of milk, one spoon of sugar and enough spoons of coffee to give the milk a little color and a roasted flavor under the sweetness. I planned to save the percolator until after Mama had gone to work and I could sit at the table and sip while I looked out the windows, like Mama sometimes did on Saturday mornings with her glass of juice while I washed dishes.

He was at the kitchen table, his legs spread out. He wasn't one of the ones who barely looked at me on their way in or out but Joe Henry, the nice one, the only one who came by during the day. He was as tall as Uncle Frank and looked a little like him, too, except his eyes were wider, friendlier and he smiled a lot. He broke into a huge grin when he saw me. "Hey, there, Baby Girl. Glad to be home?" he said. "Here." He reached into the back pocket of his shorts and folded my hand around a crumpled bill. "Go get me a paper down the street."

"No, I'll go," Mama said, reaching for my hand.

Joe Henry lifted his arm, putting it between Mama and me. "She found her way here all the way from—Where you was at?"

"Meridian."

" . . . Meridian by herself with twenty dollars but she can't go down half a block to the corner store for a newspaper? Shirl, please. Go 'head, girl. Y'all got cream? Get some half and half, too," he said, pushing another bill into my fist. And when I got back, after checking to see that Mama's back was turned while she stirred the scrambled eggs, he winked at me and folded my hand around the change. "For the next time you need to run," he whispered.

"Sit down," Mama said. "Well, your father said—"

"Dad called?"

"Don't interrupt me."

"Sorry," I said quietly. Joe Henry shook his head at the newspaper.

"He told me when I called that he was not sending you back because he and that cow could do better for you than I could." She snorted. "They can't keep track of you and they were going to keep you? I don't see how they found a place with doorways wide enough to stuff her through." She laughed. "I need to get ready for work. You go over to Mother Dear's while I'm gone."

"Can I stay here?" She gave me a sour look. "I'll go over for lunch . . . I can take care of myself okay."

She opened her mouth and I expected to hear No but she looked at Joe Henry, thought a little and said, "If you can get home on your own, I guess you can."

. . .

I got paper and pencils to write Miss Alice to warn her not to leave Yolanda with Mister Tom because he would do something, but I didn't know her address. If I wrote Yolanda, Philipa might think she helped me or knew where I was now. I put away the paper and got a book to read. When I got sleepy and bored inside, I sat on the porch to read. It was hot and a few times my sweat dripped onto the book. The few kids on the block were either in summer school or inside out of the heat. It finally made me sleepy again and I went back inside, tired and bored. I lay on my bed to read.

"Wake the hell up!"

Mama shook my leg and slapped my arm. I got up.

"I didn't mean to . . ."

"What? Lay around all day like there's somebody taking care of you? Is that what you did in Meridian all day, sleep? I'm giving you chores and you *will* go to Mother Dear's." She talked while she changed in the bathroom and went to the kitchen. "I send you so you're not here all summer doing nothing, so I don't have to spend money I do not have that's just expensive babysitting for a child too old to be watched and what does that son-of-a-bitch do? Now I'm stuck with this idiot and he's scot-free. Again! What the fuck are you looking at?" she said to me. "Put some water in that pot and get it boiling." After I put the lid on, she said, "Did you put salt in?"

"Do you want me to?"

"No, I'm just talking to myself, yes, dummy, put salt in the water. You never did have much common sense to speak of." She said the last part to herself but I heard her. Instead of feeling guilty, I got mad. I'd gotten myself home with no help, from her anyway. And she was starting to sound like Philipa—impossible to satisfy, always mad.

We didn't talk unless she wanted me to do something. After I washed and put away the dishes and pots, Mama made a weekly list of chores, something for me to do every day. Tomorrow I was to go to Mother Dear's and clean her whole house. Wednesdays were for laundry, ours and Mother Dear's, Thursdays to clean our house, Fridays to do whatever chores Mother Dear needed done. "And I can watch you on weekends," Mama said as she taped the piece of paper on my bedroom door.

"Watch me for what?"

"Go to bed."

. . .

Mother Dear gave me a box of Q-Tips to dust the crannies of her dressing table even though she just used it to pile newspapers on. Then I had to sweep the floors and beat the rugs, Mother Dear watching the whole time I dragged the rolled-up rugs out, hoisted them over the front fence and beat them with an old wood broom almost as heavy as the rugs. My bath water that night before dinner was gray and my muscles burned.

"You're quiet. You must be good and tired," Mama said.

The phone rang. I picked it up. "Hello."

"Why hello there—"

Philipa's voice. I hung up.

"Who was it?" Mama called from the front room.

"Didn't say."

"Finish the dishes," she said with a yawn. "I'm tired."

I spent Wednesday morning at Mother Dear's, doing her laundry, Mother Dear making a few loads of laundry into ten, with something to hang on the line in each load. And I couldn't leave until all the clothes were dry, so I hung them in the hot sun where they dried quickly. She frowned as she felt the shirts and sheets she hadn't wanted "torn up" in the dryer. "Better not be faded," she said. They weren't. She called Mama at work to say I was doing a good job. Whatever Mama said made her look at me and laugh.

. . .

"Mama? Do I get an allowance in summer?"

She was ready for work and opening all the kitchen cabinets. "Take down all these dishes and dust them off. And put them back the right way. Now, what you say?"

"Do I get an allowance in the summer?"

"Allowance? What for?" On her way out she called back in, "And sweep this porch off."

I dusted and put back all the dishes in the top of the cabinets—china with blueberries in the center and green leaves around the gold-trimmed edges, plates and bowls of all sizes, dishes we never used, not even at Thanksgiving. Mama said they were from when she and Dad were married and we'd never used them then, either, though to other people she said she won them at the grocery store, and Dear told a complete other story, that they were her dishes she just didn't have room for and Dad left Mama before they could get married. I was filling the bucket with hot water to clean the floors when the phone rang. I thought it might be Mama, checking. "Hello."

"Little bitch, don't—"

Philipa. I hung up. The phone rang again and I let it. I didn't have to listen to her. She was there and I was here with Mama. But I thought of Miss Alice, and the bus ride, how I could go anywhere, and that if I finished the house I could walk to the park or the library and be back before Mama got home.

I locked the door, hung the key around my neck and swept the dust off the porch into the bushes.

I walked very slowly by Mother Dear's, slow enough so if she saw me I could pretend I was going into her yard. When I reached the corner, out of sight, I ran sweating to the park three blocks away. The fence had big holes cut in it and instead of walking around to the open gate, I went through one of the holes. I wasn't afraid like Mama told me I should be. She said it was dangerous there but all I could see was paint peeling off the swings, slide and monkey bars. The pool had been closed for years and chains and two padlocks held the doors to the green and blue building closed but the fence around the pool had been cut dozens of times and was barely standing. Of the four swings, one had been wrapped tight around the upper bar, one was wood and broken almost in half. I stood on a swing and just watched cars pass the block. The whole time I was there, not one kid came or walked by. It was so empty I expected Yolanda to walk up behind me and demand I braid her Barbie's hair.

. . .

Mama seemed happier with me, the house clean and laundry done and nothing for her to do on the weekend but cook. She sat on the sofa and smiled at me. "Well, you're finally being useful," she said, laughing. When I didn't laugh, she pursed her lips and shook her head. "No common sense and no sense of humor," she said to herself but I heard her. I waited for Monday to come and her to go to work. I counted the weeks on the calendar until school started but then I thought she would be so happy about me doing all this housework for her and Mother Dear that even with homework I'd still have to clean both houses and do everyone's laundry and dust the china every week. Mama let me spend the rest of the day in my room because she thought I was reading a book. Mostly, I felt more unloved than in Meridian. Here they were supposed to love me, not my chores. And then I cried a little while, missing Mamalita, thinking I'd never see Dad again, that Dad never wanted to see me again, if he was listening to Philipa and I knew he was.

. . .

I did chores and sneaked off to the park every day. Mama whipped me once for saying Mother Dear gave me clean clothes to wash and hang as busywork. Mama had a green plastic paddle missing the ball and string; on it in big yellow letters was "SOCK

IT TO ME!" and it stung but didn't leave marks. I checked in the bathroom, using Mama's hand mirror so I could see my behind and it was as pale as ever, a little flushed but that faded even while I was looking. I wished she'd leave some marks I could show Mamalita.

I was sweeping the porch when a cab pulled up. I thought it was the older lady across the street coming back from the store or the doctor, she used a cab a couple times a month, and I waved so she wouldn't tell Mama I had been rude. The driver got out, opened the trunk and placed two big suitcases by our bottom step. He didn't look at me. The back door opened. And Yolanda jumped out, wearing a huge, deep-dimpled smile, tiny shorts and a shirt that didn't cover her stomach, Barbie and Ken in hand. She bounced up our steps and grabbed me in a hug.

"Mama said I could bring you your clothes and visit awhile," Yolanda said.

"Mama won't let you stay here," I said.

"It was so boring when you left. Now we can have some fun." She dragged the suitcases up to the porch. I felt sick. Mama would never believe I didn't tell Yolanda to come. I wondered if Dad or Philipa would still be in the townhouse tonight when Mama called.

We sat on the porch with Yolanda's suitcases. She wanted to play Barbies but I kept looking down the street, waiting for Mama's car to turn the corner and slide into the parking space in front. At least the house was clean. Mama could only get so mad if the house was clean, I hoped.

Mama came up with a smile. "So who's your friend?"

"Hi Mama," Yolanda said.

Mama looked at her like her head was on backwards. Then she saw the suitcases. "What in the hell is going on here?" she said.

"Mama said I could visit," Yolanda said.

"Mama? Mama who? Who the fuck are you?"

"This is Yolanda."

Mama looked at us awhile then started shaking her head, slowly at first then faster as she went inside saying, "Oh, no, one child is too much but another . . ."

"She's nice," Yolanda said.

"No, she's not."

"She not?"

"Why did you call her Mama?"

"You called mine Mama so I'll call yours Mama," she said, smiling.

"Get in here!"

I jumped and ran inside. Yolanda stayed on the porch with the dolls and suitcases. I told Mama the number and she called but got no answer. She called again and again. She forgot I was there and looked at the screen door, shook her head some more then noticed me and said, "Did I tell you to come in here?"

"Yes."

"Go start dinner," she said.

I heard her talking sweetly to Yolanda and Yolanda's happy chirps back, but when Mama came in the kitchen her face was sour. She told me to get out, leave her to cook dinner, and try calling Dad and Philipa again. I had Yolanda call. No answer. Yolanda thought she knew Philipa's work number but at the number she called, no one had heard of Philipa. At dinner mostly Yolanda talked. I felt like a tree had crashed into the house.

• • •

With Yolanda I could clean our house faster but Dear had us working harder on the days we went to hers—weeding the sidewalk in the yard and right in front of the door, chopping between the squares of concrete with a hand shovel to get the grass and lanky dandelions out, cleaning the shed floor with a hose and push broom, pulling all the weeds out of the grass in a yard twice the size of the five-room shotgun and, when we were drippy with sweat, she had us come in the house, ice cold with all three air conditioners on high, to flip her mattress and dust with Q-Tips the crannies in the broken console TV she used as a dressing table. But since I wasn't alone, I could call Mama at work or ask Mother Dear if we could go to the park. We got permission to go to the park and went to the library instead. I showed Yolanda how to look for her dad's name in the library phone books. At home she tried calling. She never cried or got upset about it. I guess she felt she had a place to live, that Mama wouldn't send her off like everyone else had. When she called me her sister, the skin on my back crawled.

"Isn't there anybody else?" I said to Yolanda. We had tried to play at the park but it was too hot, even under the big live oaks sharing a snowball, and we were on the porch, folding red construction paper into fans.

"Like who?"

"Somebody else who knows where your mom is or your dad or grandmother or Miss Alice or somebody."

"I guess I got nobody but you, Sandi."

I didn't say anything else. I felt heavy in the chest and my face got hot, like I was blushing. Little wafts of air floated over from Yolanda's fan.

Mama parked in front of the house. "Hey, Yolanda, hey Sandi." My scalp crawled because it was bad enough that Mama always said hi to Yolanda first but also after eight years of being Sandrine, in two weeks I had become Sandi and it grated like a rusty metal file whether they joked or not about me being sandy-colored.

She smiled at Yolanda and said, "Why didn't y'all turn on the air conditioner in the living room and sit in there? It's too hot today."

"Because you told me never to turn on that air conditioner," I said.

"Don't be such a dummy," she said to me, glancing at Yolanda to see what she thought. "Why would I want you to be this hot?"

"I don't know, why would you?" I heard myself say. Yolanda nudged me with her elbow and I snatched my arm away. "Cut it out," I said.

"I have had more than enough—"

"Then get rid of me again."

She grabbed my arm and dragged me to her bed. She took "Sock It To Me" out of her top dresser drawer.

"I hate you," I said.

Mama stopped, paddle in mid-swing. "What did you say?"

"I hate you." She raised her arm higher and hit me on the back as hard as she could. My skin stung under the shirt but as she hit me on the arms and legs and back and butt I kept talking. "You talk to Yolanda like she's sugar and treat me like you hate me and that's why I hate you."

"Take it back."

"No!"

She pushed me down on the bed and hit me on the butt harder and faster. "Take it back!" I buried my face in the bedspread. I wanted to stop breathing but I couldn't manage it.

"Mama!" Yolanda. "Mama, please, please stop, I'll go, I will, please stop!"

I don't know if Yolanda surprised her or what but Mama stopped. I went to my room and closed the door but I didn't want them coming in and there was no lock so I pushed the dresser in front of the door. When I was finally safe, like it was the first time I'd been safe all summer, I cried until dark. And when I got tired I crawled into bed, still wearing my clothes and sandals.

In the morning I was ready to go to the bathroom until I smelled eggs and bacon. Yolanda couldn't cook. It was Mama though no friend had stayed over. She was cooking breakfast for Yolanda on a weekday, something she never did for me though she said she used to when she and Dad were still together. Let her keep Yolanda, I thought. Nobody wanted Yolanda but Mama. And everybody but Mama wanted me, but that wasn't true. Dad was gone. Any aunt or uncle would send me back when she said so or got tired of cleaning the house herself and doing her own laundry.

A knock. Another knock. "Sandi?" Mama said. "I'm going to work. Open the door."

"Aw, go away," I said, not loud enough for her to hear.

"Sandi? You want some eggs?" Yolanda said.

I wasn't coming out for a breakfast she'd cooked for a child not even hers; she'd said she didn't want her own, but she could want Yolanda. I looked in my closet. I knew what I'd take if I had to go. I'd done it once, I could do it again and again forever. I loved no one. But Mamalita.

Mama didn't go to work. I heard her on the phone, I heard Yolanda sweeping the floor, I even heard Mother Dear knocking and calling at the door and I wished it was Mamalita so I could go home with her. She loved me. She made me jelly and custard ice cream, I had a bed to myself and a library card there. I was done with Mama. Except for an allowance since I'd need a bus ticket.

I got pen and paper and sat Indian-style on my bed. I always did my homework in the kitchen but after Meridian, I was not washing dishes for meals not cooked for me. I wrote a letter to Mamalita. I told her about Philipa hitting me, about Yolanda trying to flush away the books and how I'd let down Miss Augustine, and, though I wasn't sure exactly, I told her Mister Tom had put his thing in my mouth and made me throw up and I couldn't drink milk anymore because the taste made me remember and made me sick, I told her I ran away, I told her Yolanda came, I told her I didn't love Mama anymore and when I heard from her, I'd catch the bus to go to her.

It was almost night. I pushed the dresser away from the door.

Yolanda chirped to Mama in the kitchen. I tiptoed into the living room to get a stamp from Mama's dresser and walked out the front door, without my key, without Mama or Yolanda hearing me. I felt better outside taking deep breaths of everyone's dinner—greens, pork chops, sausage, liver, garlic and onions, cigarette smoke. I walked to the mailbox at Broad and St. Bernard and put my letter in.

• • •

I said as little to Mama and Yolanda as I could, mostly yes or no. I didn't play Barbies; nothing was fun because I was waiting. Yolanda got lonely and quiet. Mama stopped looking at me with a hard face but I still wouldn't talk to her. If I told her what I was thinking, she'd whip me for sure.

I waited another week. Mama cooked breakfast every morning before work and I ate just enough to stop the pains in my stomach. Soon I'd be eating biscuits and grits and hard-rind bacon and homemade jelly every morning for the rest of my life. In church on Sunday I stood, kneeled, said words without thinking about them until it was time to go home and even though I usually couldn't wait for Lent each year because once a week our class did the Stations of the Cross and I could look at the stained-glass windows showing the Mysteries up close, the paper-white Jesus, the drops of blood, Mary's face turned up to heaven, begging God to save her son just for her, no other reason, just because she loved Him and wanted Him, I didn't even glance at the windows and didn't care about any of it.

Mama sat near me on the sofa while we watched Flip Wilson on TV. The phone rang and I jumped. By Mama's tone, I knew it was Dad.

"Is it Mama?" Yolanda said.

"Sandi. Your father."

"Dad?"

"Hey, cream pie."

"I wrote Mamalita."

"Mamalita. I didn't tell you, she's been sick. That's why I didn't . . ." He sighed, sounding like a loud gust and my heart almost stopped. "I'm sorry."

I didn't want Mama and Yolanda to hear I had expected her to send for me. "That's okay, I can see her next summer, can't I?"

"Pie." Another gusty sigh and my heart did stop. "I'm really sorry. Mamalita is gone."

My throat burned. "Gone where?"

"Gone gone, pie."

My eyes were open but everything went black. I heard the phone hit the floor, felt myself walk to my room. I got in bed, pulled the covers over my head.

I stayed in bed for days. I had no eyes or ears, I had no stomach, I couldn't feel my arms or legs, everything was gone. I wanted Mama to kill me but I knew she wouldn't, not now when I needed her to. Mother Dear came in my room each day, I knew because I could smell her Shalimar, but I couldn't see anything. Everything was gone. And I had nowhere to go.

• • •

"... please, you want what's
Mamalita's house."

I opened my eyes or I s
tunnel. It was Mama talkin
the bed. I didn't touch it u
room. Rag dolls Mamalita l
outgrown, the *Little House* (
mer. And at the bottom, th
written on the labels: "For
held one up to the window
amber. I opened it, dipped i
Mamalita talking to me.

I had to take care of myself. And I could. I had plenty of common sense. I could even take care of Yolanda if I had to. Only I
understood, not Mama or Yolanda, that Philipa would never want
Yolanda back. And Yolanda would be better off without her.

I put the box in my closet and hid two of the jelly jars in the
drawer with my underwear and shirts. I went to the kitchen and,
with Mama and Yolanda and Mother Dear watching, made and
ate one pomegranate jelly sandwich.

2

Mama said she had told Dad that Yolanda would be ready whenever they came. I wondered why she was so nice about it but I didn't think meanness would've made them come either. Yolanda kept her clothes in her suitcase, put her toys in it every night, said "Thank you" and "Please" a lot, all gratefulness. I knew they wouldn't come. Like Miss Alice said, it was their honeymoon and they wanted to be alone.

I started talking to Mama again but in my head didn't think of her as "Mama" anymore; she was "Shirleen." I slipped and called her Mama sometimes when talking to Yolanda but I didn't slip around Shirleen; I called her Mama or nothing. And Shirleen changed. She cooked breakfast in the morning before work. She had fewer hard looks, at me or Yolanda, and even had a soft, sorry look when Yolanda couldn't see her face. As school got closer and closer, I think Shirleen realized Dad and Philipa were not coming for Yolanda. At least I was wanted; I just didn't want the people who wanted me.

I dreamed about Mamalita's house most nights. I felt safe and warm asleep, cold, alone and stiff awake. Yolanda chirped and bubbled all day and until I fell asleep, except at Dear's house where she was quiet and watched with big eyes and kept looking over her shoulder for Dear.

"Just stop it," I said. We were on the floor with the Q-Tips, dusting the roses and leaves carved into the legs of Dear's coffee table, saving the used Q-Tips in a plastic bowl for Dear to inspect; the day before, she'd inspected them and decided we didn't use enough to get the carvings really clean so we were at it again today. "It's not like she's your mother or anything," I said.

"But she's so mean," Yolanda whispered, tickling my ear with her soft breath, hot in the over-air-conditioned house.

"And the more you show her you're scared of her, the meaner she gets. Trust me. I know." Until I was seven, I had to go to Dear's house after school. I wasn't allowed to play outside, watch TV, make noise, or draw because drawing might leave marks on the table or eraser crumbs on the floor. When I moped at the windows, watching the kids from down the block, Dear told me I was spoiled, that it was time for me to learn to work for my keep, that I better stop pouting or she would give me something to pout about. But when I came in without one backward look, when I stayed away from the windows and sat reading, trying to be as quiet and still as possible, Dear didn't even come in the room and eventually let me sit on the porch. Misery to her was the same as disobedience.

Yolanda pulled in her lower lip and kept cleaning. When Dear saw her long face over the bowl of used Q-Tips, instead of sending us to the yard to pick weeds along the fence, she made us clean the bathroom on our hands and knees with hot water and ammonia, every crease in the feet of the bathtub, every inch behind the toilet, even the frosted window I had to balance on the rounded edge of the claw-foot tub to reach. "See?" I said to Yolanda as we squeezed out the sponges. My hands were dark pink about to go red, what they always did when I cleaned with ammonia and I knew Dear wouldn't have made us do it if Yolanda hadn't sulked so much. Shirleen gasped when she saw my hands at dinner, slathered Vaseline on and covered them with mittens. I could barely hold a fork.

• • •

Two Sundays before school started, Shirleen, Yolanda and I walked to church and stopped at the K&B afterwards. Smelling the sweetness, I felt a little happier inside. I had strawberry ice cream, Yolanda a root beer float, Shirleen a fudge sundae. We sat in a booth. Yolanda was all thank yous and smiles, still grateful like she thought Philipa would be coming for her tomorrow.

Shirleen cleared her throat. "Ice cream made my throat all cold." Yolanda giggled. Shirleen gave a little smile then became serious, not a stern serious but a gentle kind. "School starts in two weeks," she said.

Next to me in the booth, Yolanda kept sipping and scooping as if no one had spoken. Shirleen turned more towards her. "School starts in two weeks," she said again. "And I think, Yolanda, we should register you at Sandi's school."

Yolanda looked up, squinting, then she looked into her float glass. She shivered, like she could feel Philipa wasn't coming for her soon, maybe never.

Shirleen finished her sundae. "We'll have to take you over there this week to see what grade you should be in. Get you uniforms. I could probably take in Sandi's from last year …"

"And what will I wear?"

"You need a new set, Sandi. Did you think I'd let you go naked?" I was too mad to answer and she stopped smiling. "So, should we get some school supplies?"

I felt happy carrying home my own bag of loose-leaf and

graph paper, pencils, pens, notebooks, and colored pencils. Yolanda hugged her bag of supplies to her chest. She had less since Shirleen wasn't sure which grade she'd be in and what exactly she'd need. I didn't think Yolanda had ever gone to school regularly. When I asked her at home, she didn't answer.

• • •

I walked Yolanda to St. John of God to meet the sisters and take a test. There were three shallow steps and a huge arching doorway with Latin words over the arch and the entryway was dark and cool like a cave. I waited outside, on the front steps, facing the church across the street. From outside, the stained glass windows looked black and without detail. I wondered if Yolanda was even Catholic. Even though I loved the stained glass windows and the incense and the poinsettias on the altar at Christmas and the Stations of the Cross at Lent and dipping my fingertips in lukewarm holy water, I was becoming pretty sure there was no God. I'd have to ask Yolanda what she thought.

A red car passed very slowly, the man driving with his arm out the window, hand on the side mirror. The car circled the block and came back and parked in front of the school. Without turning my face, I looked to see if I recognized him, a friend of Shirleen's, a neighbor, someone's father.

"School start soon, huh?" he called out.

"Next week." He had dark skin but his eyes were pale, grayish, and then I recognized him, a friend of Shirleen's, one who'd been at the party after I came home but not one of the faces I occasionally saw when I opened my door or stepped out the bathroom in the morning. I couldn't remember his name but I always remembered his funny-colored eyes since last March when Shirleen's car broke down and he spent the week driving her to work—the one day it rained and Shirleen said I could still walk, it wasn't a hard rain, he'd shook his head at her and opened the door for me to get in the cluttered back seat of his car—and I'd see him when I walked home from school under Shirleen's car or bent over the open hood. He wasn't like Joe Henry, dashikied Raheem, Albert or Jonnie, not a friend I saw every month, sometimes three mornings in a row, but a friend she'd let in if he dropped by on a boring evening with a six-pack and none of her usual friends were around. I couldn't remember ever seeing him in the morning though he could've left before I woke.

"You waiting on that girl you walked with?"

I scooted backwards on the stair, my back straight. "Yeah. She'll be done soon," I said.

"Now that's nice ... Kids don't watch out for each other like they used to," he said. "Anybody can tell you not sisters. Nothing in your faces the same."

I was surprised he didn't call us salt and pepper, like Dear did. Then I wondered how he knew I'd walked her to St. John's. I was ready to run inside to find Yolanda when she came out and sat next to me.

"Y'all be careful going home, huh?"

"Yes, sir." He smiled when I said "sir" and drove away nodding and waving the hand resting on the side mirror.

"I gotta do second grade again," Yolanda said.

"You did it before?"

"I'm eight, right?"

"A birthday isn't the same as a whole grade."

She got up and started walking, the wrong way. "Yolanda! This way." She turned and followed me with her head down.

• • •

Yolanda blended in at school like she had always been there. By the end of the first week, you couldn't pick her out as new or different, her chocolate skin firmly in place with the ambers, cinnamons, and milk and dark chocolates around her in identical red, gray and white plaid skirts and thin white shirts. Though I had been there since age five, I was the one who stood out. Even on the first day of the year, when girls hugged and squealed and talked with their heads close together, only Yolanda paid attention to me. From the girls in my class I got tight, polite smiles or single nods of the head. Shirleen had told me to walk Yolanda to Sister Lawrence's room but she was surrounded by girls from the time we got to the front stairs and they took her to Sister Lawrence's second floor room. I went to the sixth grade room, Miss Boudreaux, the only non-sister in the school, like Mister Albert was the only non-priest. She had relaxed hair she wore in a bun on top her head, cinnamon skin, and such a light, soft voice she had to use a bell to quiet us down for the Pledge of Allegiance and prayers. I took a desk by the window, like I had since third grade, hoping the sunlight would darken me to at least a pancake color. Then I wouldn't stand out so much against the chocolates, caramels, cinnamons and ambers around me all day.

Every day we saw the red car, either passing on Broad when we walked to school or parked near the school, especially by the yard during recess. The sisters had the yard divided for recess, girls on the side nearest the street and lined on one end by a wooden walkway we used to get from the school to the cafeteria when it rained but the boys' side was bigger, had a baseball diamond painted on the asphalt, a basketball hoop and a couple of trees for shade. When I'd described his car, Shirleen called him "Champ" and he watched at recess, especially the older girls who never ran but stood in the walkway talking, passing notes, and looking at their hair in little mirrors kept in their purses.

The dozen white kids at the school didn't sit aside like I

did. The boys played together like no one was different, and the white girls stood in their own groups doing the same talking, note-passing and mirror-looking as the black girls. I got straight As; not even white kids talked to me.

. . .

I gave away my milk for three weeks before Sister Mary Clare saw me pass it down our table of fifth- and sixth-grade girls. At the tray cart and garbage can, she put a full carton of milk on my tray and told me to drink it.

"Milk makes me sick, Sister," I said.

"Not only does your mother pay good money for this lunch, but there are children all over the world and in this city who are starving and would be grateful for that one carton of milk."

"It makes me sick, Sister." My voice trembled; I could already taste vanilla, raisins, sharp sour vomit.

Her pinkish face pinched into impatience. "Drink that milk, Sandrine Miller."

I emptied my tray, holding onto the milk, and while girls and boys walked around me to throw out garbage and stack their trays, I drank the milk. The first sip reminded me of salty, sour vomit so I pinched my nose and drank it as fast as I could. Sister gave me a satisfied smile. I felt a little dizzy, my stomach heavy like it was filled with glue. Mister Albert, the seventh-grade teacher, stood by the doorway. When I got close enough to smell the cigarette smoke on him, I threw up all over his pants.

I felt better with the milk out but Sister Mary Clare insisted I go home. She called Shirleen from the principal's office. Next she called Mother Dear to come and get me.

"Yes," she said to Mother Dear. "No, I do think she should come home. How soon can . . . What?" Sister Mary Clare straightened up and looked around the office. "But the child has been sick." She listened a little longer then hung up. "Sandrine, your grandmother says if you're coming home, you are walking alone. Do you feel well enough?"

"I'd rather stay here."

"I agree, I don't think you should be walking right now."

The next day Sister Mary Clare made me drink milk again and I threw up at the doorway where Mister Albert had been the day before. The day after I threw up into the garbage can. Friday Shirleen came to get me and spent a few minutes in the principal's office with Sisters Mary Clare and Paul. When she came out she said, "I guess you won't be drinking milk at school anymore."

"I told Sister Mary Clare I'd be sick."

Her car was right in front of the school. "That never happened before." Champ's red car passed. "When did that start?"

I watched the car turn the corner. "Champ's here."

"With milk, Sandi, focus, please."

I was looking behind us to see if he would circle the block or had passed by chance but then he came around the block and parked by the schoolyard. The seventh and eighth grade girls had PE after lunch. He stopped his motor and slid over to the passenger side where he could see the yard better. "There he is," I said. Shirleen's eyes looking at me got narrower and she didn't look behind us or in the rearview mirror.

"What are you so worried about him for? He don't have any kids at this school."

"Then what's he doing here all the time?"

Shirleen looked at me carefully like she was trying to see something inside me. "You come straight home after school—"

"I always do."

"Don't talk back! You come straight home after school, you hear me?"

Champ was leaning on the passenger side door, chin on his crossed arms as he watched the girls play volleyball, their net the line on the pavement dividing the boys and girls sides of the yard.

I said, "Yeah, yeah."

. . .

I waited for Yolanda outside school. The other kids streamed out with mothers or to mothers in cars lined up at the curb. In a few minutes it was all quiet, just traffic whispering on Broad St.

The red car turned the corner and parked in front of the stairs, right in front of me reading my science textbook. I had looked at the questions at the end of every chapter the first day of school and realized I could answer most of them correctly without reading anything. I wanted to read the whole book and answer all the questions that weekend so I'd just have to turn in homework when it was due.

Champ's funny-colored eyes were pointed down. When I looked at him, I smelled sour milk and got a chill up my back. I sat up straighter and wrapped my skirt around my knees.

"Where your friend?"

I put my nose back in the book. "Inside."

"Her skirts getting short. She must be having a growth spurt like they say."

I heard shuffling behind me and closed the book right before Yolanda walked out, holding her books on top of her head. She had homework every night but usually watched the Three Stooges and the Little Rascals until Shirleen came home. I let her step out into the sun and looked. He was right; her skirts were shorter than the first week of school.

"They were mine," I said. "Maybe that's why she's outgrowing them."

Champ didn't answer. He was looking at me and Yolanda but not at our faces. Yolanda spun around and around, her skirt twirling higher. His smile made a bitter taste creep into my mouth. "C'mon, Yolanda," I said. She twirled a few more times then started to follow me. Champ drove close to the curb alongside us.

"Y'all going home, huh? Got homework?"

I felt Yolanda slow down. "Yeah," I said and pulled Yolanda's arm to make her walk faster.

"Hey, y'all want a ride?"

Yolanda looked up and stopped walking.

"No," I said.

"C'mon, it's hot. I got air condition in here. I get you some ice cream, too."

"No," I said.

"C'mon, get in. Shirl know. I told her I'd pick y'all up sometimes. 'Specially a day like this one, it's some hot for late September."

I grabbed Yolanda's arm and walked faster. We stopped at the corner and so did he. The light was green. He turned the corner enough to stop the car right in front of us and leaned over to his passenger door just as I pulled Yolanda around the car and across the street. I knew walking against traffic would make it harder for him to follow us. I walked fast, Yolanda trotting to keep up. She didn't complain even though I dragged her the whole eleven blocks home. I asked her later if she would've gotten in the car. "He was just gonna give us a ride," she said.

"No, he wasn't."

"He wasn't?"

"Not the way you think."

"Oh."

• • •

The red car was parked at the end of our block. I told Yolanda we'd walk a different way.

"It's okay," Yolanda said. "He probably just wants to give us a ride or something."

"Please," I said.

As we passed, Champ called out, "Yolanda! Hey, you want a ride?"

Before she could answer, I said, "No!"

"Damn, you rude," he said. "You don't have to be rude. You think your mama want to hear 'bout it?"

"Leave us alone."

"Stuck-up yella bitch, I ain't talking to you, I'm talking to the pretty one so get your ugly white ass to school!"

My stomach heaved but I was angry. I took Yolanda's arm and walked the opposite way. We took an alternate route, against traffic and up one-way streets until we had to cross Broad St. to get to St. John's.

• • •

Before recess, while the other sixth-grade girls giggled and talked over and around me and brushed down stray hairs, I looked at my face in the mirror—the color of the insides of vanilla wafers, hardly a color at all, lips wide and tall and pink, brown eyes and almost-black hair the darkest things on me. The other girls were starting to look like teenagers while I looked like I'd been skipped two years and didn't belong. All the girls suddenly left and in the empty and quiet I heard blood pulsing in my ears.

I went outside to the yard. When school first began, I was glad Yolanda didn't have recess at the same time as me but almost all the girls in my class were done with playing at recess; they shared magazines or showed each other makeup in their purses that they were not allowed to wear at school but put on as they walked home, always a few blocks away so none of the sisters saw them. But it wasn't about playing; the black girls, thinking I was stuck up because I was lighter, got good grades and went straight home after school, didn't talk to me while the white girls in the sixth, seventh and eighth grades didn't talk to me because I wasn't white. With Yolanda I could at least play tag or Mary Mack or hopscotch.

· · ·

Looking at the church across the street, I wondered if Mister Tom would go to hell. Then I saw the red car in the church parking lot and wondered if Champ would go to hell, too, for what he was thinking. Or what he would end up doing to stupid Yolanda or someone else who got in his car.

The second grade was on the second floor, at the end closest to the back stairs. Yolanda sat in a desk, writing. Sister Lawrence came to sit next to her and checked the paper, patting Yolanda on the back. Yolanda looked angry and sad. Sister Lawrence had a piercing, cackling laugh and, after Sister Agnes, the kindergarten teacher, was probably the kindest sister at the school. I'd loved second grade with her. The work was easy and she'd let me sit in the back and read once I'd finished my work. When I helped kids who sat around me, she gave me a big smile and a bookmark with a saint or prayer on it. I also got to read part of the gospel at school Mass once, something no second grader had ever done. The three kids who liked me turned on me after that, like I thought I was too good for them instead of them thinking I was too good for them.

Sister Lawrence put Yolanda's papers away, gave her two more and turned to erase the board. Yolanda picked up her books like they were cement and loped to the door. She didn't see me at the door and walked to the stairs.

By the time we got outside, the red car was parked right in front of the school. Yolanda was too upset to notice or say anything dumb. As we passed the car, Champ flicked and waggled his pink tongue at us; I knew he meant something by it but I didn't know what. I looked for something to throw at him but I was afraid that if we stopped, he might think we did want a ride or candy or whatever he would offer today and if I did throw a rock at his car, even though he hadn't seen Shirleen for weeks as far as I knew, he was sure to tell her his side of the story. I told myself in my head, like I was talking to one of the dark brown girls at school, that he was creepy, that he couldn't be trusted, that I was not running from him because he was dark. It made me tired, my fists clenched like I really was talking to someone, her eyes half-closed with boredom, an eye roll or suck of the teeth before sashaying off and laughing at me with her friends. I had to defend myself everywhere; with Mamalita in summers, I'd needed no guard to pull over my head.

While Yolanda helped Shirleen with dishes, I looked in her books and folders. Her spelling papers had Ds and Fs, her math papers had Cs and her religion papers were blank with Fs on them. I wondered if Shirleen would be angry like when I got a single C in religion last year, just because I kept asking Father McNeeley why girls couldn't be altar boys, or if Shirleen would get that soft, sorry look. I felt sorry for Yolanda now, too. Her father didn't want her, her mother didn't want her, she didn't have a family or school of her own, she had to share mine not knowing when it would end.

$$\bullet \quad \bullet \quad \bullet$$

Miss Boudreaux pulled me aside before recess to tell me not to raise my hand so much in class; she said I always knew the answer and should give others a chance. I felt ashamed and angry and wanted to tell Shirleen but thinking of her answer deflated my anger and increased the shame; she would say whatever was wrong was my fault and she had never come to school to talk to a teacher and wouldn't start now. I nodded my head to Miss Boudreaux but thought I'd fall asleep without something to do, even just raising my hand. I had finished all the science book questions and written them neatly with a blank line for the date I needed to turn them in.

I looked forward every day to math class—Miss Boudreaux had asked Sister Paul, the principal, to put me in another math class so every afternoon, I walked up to the third floor, to Mr. Albert's seventh-grade math class. The seventh-grade girls wouldn't talk to me in class but Mr. Albert was strict about talking and I never expected them to. They were almost teenagers, carried purses and lip gloss, ate lunch together, had PE together. The only time we saw an older girl was at recess, when Sister Michael had one come down to watch the girls' side of the yard. Mr. Albert didn't tell me to not raise my hand; he had me come to the board, gave me nods and extra points for doing extra questions. I thought about showing Miss Boudreaux all the science questions I'd answered to see if she'd send me to the third floor for science, too.

• • •

The other boys and girls got loud during art and Miss Boudreaux rang her bell just as Sister Paul walked by. Sister Paul gave us all detention. I raised my hand to tell her I had to walk Yolanda home but she ignored my hand. I didn't get to tell Yolanda I'd be late. I watched the clock and door the whole hour of detention.

Yolanda was not on the front steps or in the yard. I walked across the street into the cool dark church to look. I tiptoed up and down the outer aisles, not looking at the windows but knowing by the spots of color on the floor and my arms what

Stations I passed. I wanted to look, I still loved the windows but I didn't believe in God or heaven or Jesus or Mary anymore, only hell and the devil and evil people.

Yolanda wasn't there. I was so scared I wanted to cry.

I stood on the school steps. "Yolanda! Yolanda!"

No answer. No red car.

I rushed home, running half the way, thinking Champ may have given Yolanda a ride home after candy or ice cream or whatever he promised her and whatever he wanted. And there she was, curled in a ball on the porch in the corner. When she saw me she smiled. I had to catch my breath.

"I didn't have a key," she said.

"Are you okay?"

"Uh-huh. You want a Mary Jane?" She held up a small paper bag.

"Where'd you get that?"

She shrugged. "He wanted a kiss, that's all."

Now I could see some hair on one side of her head was pulled out of the braid and her shirt was missing a button. The rest of her looked okay but I didn't know what to look for. "Oh, Yolanda. Now we have to tell Shirleen," I said.

"No!"

"Yes, we do because I don't know what to do now."

She started crying. "He made me kiss him, that's all, that's all, that's all."

Inside I gently combed her hair back into place. I made her tell me: When she leaned away after kissing his lips, which were dry and rough, he tried to grab her. She scrambled away from him to the door and her button popped off as she pulled away to get out of the car. Her regular smile came back and she said, "At least I got the candy!"

· · ·

Champ was parked right in front of school. He stared at me as we passed. Then his eyes slid away to a group of loud-talking sixth-grade girls who had rolled the waists of their skirts to make them shorter and folded down their socks to show as much leg as possible. They walked the opposite way. When I looked back, his head was turning back and forth between them and Yolanda and me. I hurried Yolanda around the corner and across Broad to one-way streets we could take home.

Mother Dear was on her porch when we turned the corner. She had been looking the opposite way, toward Broad, expecting us that way, and when she finally saw us she got a crooked smile on her face and said, "Here they come—salt and pepper!" She laughed then her forehead wrinkled up. "What you doing coming from that way? Where were you? What were you doing? Who was with you?"

"Nobody," I said.

"Liar!"

"I don't lie," I said. "We walked a different way because Champ was following us."

Mother Dear lunged her three hundred pounds out the chair. "I'm calling your mama."

"What for?" I said. I went next door to unlock our front door for Yolanda then went back to Mother Dear's shotgun. She said she kept it dark all year so it would be cool in the summer and I looked down the dark tunnel of the house and saw her at the far end in the lit-up kitchen, talking on the phone.

She gave me a smug half-smile. "What did you tell her?" I said.

"Uh-huh, she right here." She held out the phone and lightly bounced her head, like saying she told me so.

"You and Yolanda are to walk straight home from school, period," Shirleen said.

"We did."

"Mother Dear says you came up from Dupre instead of Broad."

"You know Champ? He's—"

"Don't start that shit about Champ. What are you doing with him anyway? He's too old for me, much less you and if I find—"

I hung up. Mother Dear still had her smug look. "So what she say?"

"Go home and do homework."

"Uh-huh, she gon' tear your behind up later."

"No she won't because I didn't do anything wrong."

"Then I'll whip your lying behind."

I snorted. "Yeah, right. Catch me."

Her cinnamon face got red and she reached for a fly swatter on the wall. I ran out the door, jumped the four stairs and was inside our house, door locked, before I figured she could get to her front door. She'd tell Shirleen. I put on shorts and a T-shirt, spread my books on the kitchen table and started my homework. Yolanda, as usual, was in front of the TV with a big plastic tumbler of orange KoolAid.

"Ow." Shirleen had just hit me on the back of the head with her hand, still holding her keys. "What'd you do that for?" I said, not looking up from my social studies homework; I was in the last section and had just started a fresh loose-leaf page for questions and answers.

"Your attitude," Shirleen said. She put the Schwegmann's bag on the counter and Yolanda started putting away the groceries. "You don't talk back to Mother Dear or me that way."

"I wasn't talking back." Yolanda behind Shirleen looked at me with big scared deer eyes. "I was telling her the truth after she falsely accused me."

"She thought you were sassing her."

"She thinks a lot of things that aren't true," I said. "We see this guy every day."

Shirleen looked at me like she'd never seen me before. "What man you see every day?"

I stomped my foot. "Can't you listen? Champ. Champ follows us, we haven't done anything but be born girls who happen to go to that school."

"He says the uniforms are cute," Yolanda said quietly.

"Yolanda," Shirleen said, "stay out of this. At her age I got my brothers and sisters ready for school, walked them to school, met with teachers, cooked dinner and did the chores and my homework and never lost or hurt one of them. You are Sandi's responsibility after school and if she leads you wrong it's her fault and she will pay the price."

I went into my room and pushed the dresser in front of the door. I had the same feeling I had in Meridian when I decided to sneak away but I couldn't; I had nowhere to go with Mamalita dead. Thinking of her, I checked the jelly jars in my drawer. They were there, still amber, still mine.

• • •

The red car sat at the end of the block, waiting. Yolanda and I went the opposite way. I looked over my shoulder as we turned the corner and the car backed down the street to follow us. I pulled Yolanda with me trying to get to the next one-way street but if Champ had backed down our street, we might not be able to get away from him.

He drove alongside us very slowly. When we crossed and went up a one-way street, he followed, ignoring the sign. A car came the right way, honked, and the woman inside yelled he was going the wrong way. When I looked, his eyes didn't leave us, didn't even glance at the woman and her car as it went around him.

"Hey, Yolanda," Champ said.

"Stop talking to us," I said.

"I didn't say, 'Hey, yella bitch,' I said, 'Hey, Yolanda,'" he said, his face screwed up like I smelled as bad as his car did, cigarettes and old beer cooked in the sun.

Yolanda walked very close to me, her arm touching mine. She seemed afraid, like she knew something about him or what he wanted. "Are you scared?" I said to her in a whisper. She nodded her head. "Then run, go around that corner and go up the other street, I'll meet you at Broad." She squeezed my hand. I thought she wouldn't go then she took off running. He sped up until she turned the corner then slowed down to be beside me again. He followed me two more blocks. I thought to myself, He is a coward.

"If I'm so white and butt-ugly, why do you follow me every day?"

He stopped the car and I ran. I thought I heard his door screech open. I ran all the way to Broad where Yolanda waited, looking in all directions for me. We held hands and ran across the street to school.

• • •

I waited for Yolanda after school in the cool darkness of the entryway. The red car wasn't there and I hadn't seen it since morning. I heard footsteps and voices, thought it was Yolanda and turned to see the seventh and eighth grade girls leaving school in a chattering pack. I couldn't believe how tall they looked, so much older than I was, and prettier. As they stepped out into the sunlight, Champ's car turned the corner and parked in the church parking lot. The girls scattered in both directions and across the church parking lot. He tried to look at them all. The group of girls crossing the parking lot stopped at the far edge. Each girl rolled the waist of her skirt to make it shorter and folded down her white socks. When they stepped off the lot and disappeared around the corner, the red car slowly crept out of the parking lot after them.

Yolanda came out with Sister Lawrence. Yolanda looked sad again.

"Hello, Sandrine," Sister Lawrence said.

"Hello, Sister Lawrence," I said. I meant it. I still liked her.

"Give this to your mother," she said, holding out a sealed envelope. "I'll see you tomorrow, Yolanda."

Yolanda was quiet the whole walk. When I turned toward the library, she didn't object, just followed with her head down, holding her books to her chest. I told her we'd look for her father's number in the phone books again. The phone books hadn't changed but I thought she'd feel better if we tried.

After dinner I gave Shirleen the letter. She opened it, read it and said, "Mm."

"What are we going to do about Yolanda?"

"About what?"

"Her parents. Finding somebody. I think she's worried about herself."

Shirleen folded the letter and sighed. "All I can do is call child welfare and they'd put her in some foster home. She's better off here with us. Send her in here. I need to talk to her."

"What was the letter about?"

"Yolanda. I want to talk to *her* so tell *her* to come in here."

I sent Yolanda into the living room and went into my bedroom. After their talk, Shirleen came into the bedroom. She forbid any TV on school days and told me to help Yolanda every night with homework. I opened my mouth to say I already wasn't allowed to watch TV after school and no, I was not going to fall behind because Yolanda was failing second grade, but Shirleen gave me such a mean look I had to say "Okay."

• • •

Yolanda caught the flu. Walking with her, talking to her, dodging Champ kept my own thoughts back—scared and on my knees in Yolanda's room, Mister Tom's dripping thing, the police officer's voice behind my back, the ache for Mamalita. I brought Yolanda's homework home but she was too sleepy and wheezy to do it. I didn't see Champ much that week. He spent more time by the school, watching girls playing volleyball at PE or walking across the church parking lot. His favorites, I think, were the older girls.

• • •

Sister Mary Clare's hand clamped on my shoulder. "Not only does your mother pay good money for this lunch, but there are children all over the world and in this city who are starving and would be grateful for those lima beans," she said, her chin up and one finger raised as if she had a long speech ahead.

"Not these lima beans they wouldn't," I said too quietly for her to hear.

She stood waiting with her arms folded. "Since you threw away most of them, go back to the line—"

"Sister—"

"—and get another spoonful." I felt her eyes on me as I went back to the line, told them what she said and came back with a huge spoonful of lima beans on my tray. "Now eat them," Sister Mary Clare said. I tried eating them one at a time but they were gritty and tasted like sour water so I chewed big mouthfuls. By the time I was done, after-lunch recess was over and I couldn't get to the bathroom to rinse my mouth.

In art that day we made rosaries. I made mine of pearly white and sky blue beads. I held it in my hand walking home, feeling like Mamalita was behind me radiating pride I could feel on my skin like the sunlight. My mouth still tasted like lima beans. I couldn't wait to brush my teeth.

I turned the corner onto our street and there was the red car. It was turned the wrong way so he could have followed me to my door. I passed the house and went around the block. He knew where we lived but I was afraid he'd get out of the car and knock on the door or ring the bell until Shirleen got home and then tell her some lie. She was so convinced I was doing something wrong and I couldn't understand what she thought.

"Where you going, yella?" he said. "Your house back there."

I turned another corner. Champ stayed close. The rosary beads dug into my skin I held them so tight. I realized my lips were moving, praying, a Hail Mary. He said more to me but I heard only the words of the prayer in my head. I opened my hand and started to pray the rosary so I wouldn't hear him.

I was back in front of the house. The red car was parked in Shirleen's spot but Champ was gone. My heart jumped. If he got into the narrow alley between our house and the fence of Mother Dear's yard or hid under the house, he could get in a window or the back door or he might be inside already where Yolanda was, alone. I heard her cough. I put my books on the porch and tiptoed into the alley. Cool damp air from under the house brushed my calves and ankles. The small patch of yard in back was empty. My heart felt better. I stopped shaking. He was trying to scare us. "Jerk," I said. I opened the back door then remembered my books on the front porch.

I was thinking about reading Yolanda's religion homework to her. She didn't know anything about the New Testament, parables, sacraments, nothing, and she could listen without getting out of bed. I was glad I had finished so much homework ahead of time; the whole two weeks Yolanda had been sick, I hadn't done anything after school but bring her lemon and honey in hot water or cough drops, read homework to her, do the dishes myself—at least I didn't have to clean Dear's house alone; she had said to wait until Yolanda was better, adding that Yolanda did a better job than I ever did, but I think she just said that to make Shirleen frown at me.

Then he was there, a few feet from the end, a big smile on his face. He wasn't wide but the alley was narrow and he filled it up, one hand on the house wall, his other fingers twisted in the link of the fence. I opened my mouth to yell at him but nothing came out.

"Hey there, yella gal. What you doing back there, huh?" I took one step back and all of a sudden Champ was closer and had my arm. "Looking for me?"

"No," I said and it barely came out. My throat felt swollen shut and I couldn't swallow.

"Uh-huh," he said in a low voice that scared me, smiling wide, funny colored eyes shining. "Just what I thought . . ."

I pulled on my arm. He pulled back so hard I bounced off the front of him, smelled smoke like something had been burning and sharp-smelling sweat. Yolanda coughed again and I wanted to scream to her but my voice was gone again.

"Come here," he said. I shook my head as he grabbed my other arm, dragged me right in front of him and grabbed the back of my neck with one hand while his other fumbled I couldn't see where because I couldn't look at his face and wouldn't look further down than the Foxy Brown on his t-shirt. "You like me, huh?" he said. "Them butter-colored girls always like me." He took my hand and put it inside the fly of his pants, the zipper scratching my wrist and arm, and I felt something hard like a rock but covered in hairy skin. I gagged so hard I stopped breathing for a few seconds.

"Yeah, sweet-pussy yella girl," he said, breathing hard. "Act like you don't like chocolate . . . Mm, yeah." He shook me, his fingers digging into the sides of my neck, his other hand moving my hand in and out of his pants and the hair felt sharp enough to cut my skin but it was the teeth of his zipper scraping my wrist and arm and I thought blood would drip onto my shoes. He started pushing me, his shoes pinching my toes and forcing me backwards. As he backed me into the little square of yard, he grabbed my other wrist, holding it with the same hand moving my wrist and hand up and down in his pants and I kicked at his hand reaching for my skirt and legs, not sure what he would do but knowing I couldn't let him. Then he hit me, an open-hand slap as hard as a punch. My mind went blank, my ear rang, I couldn't remember what was happening or where I was until I felt my panties around my knees. I tried to pull my wrists out of his hand without moving my feet so I'd stay on them. I wanted the panties down so I could run but was scared what he'd do if they were down and I felt his scratchy-dry fingertips on my knees, grabbing at the panties and I still couldn't scream but I had to because I didn't want to fall down, because I didn't want to be in the back yard with him, because I couldn't feel my feet.

"Goddammit, Sandi, where the hell you go?"

Shirleen. He snatched my hand out of his pants and zipped up. "See you later, little mama." He pushed me a little away from him as he let me go. I waited until I thought he had walked all the way out of the alley past Shirleen. I heard him but couldn't tell who he was talking to; I was looking at the red oozing scrapes on my wrist. I wanted to cut the hand off. Shirleen stomped down the alley, her eyes huge but her mouth puckered tight and hands reaching out at me. When I opened my mouth to speak, I was surprised milk didn't shoot out all over the concrete.

"Mama ..."

She grabbed me by the back of the neck same as he did and I finally screamed; I thought she was pushing me to his car until I tripped up the stairs. The bedroom door opened right before my nose smashed into it. Shirleen pushed me down on the bed and I was already crying when I felt Sock It to Me on my legs, under my skirt, on my back, even the back of my head when I curled up.

"I am not sacrificing to send you to Catholic school to be some stupid-ass slut, slut! You don't never leave Yolanda by herself so you can be some goddamn slut!"

After she called me slut the first time, she hit me harder and faster but it started not to hurt. I couldn't feel my skin, couldn't tell if the bed under me was wet from sweat or blood or if I was crying. All I could think was how to cut off that hand. The nuns said the left hand was the devil's hand, the hand that got up to mischief, the hand that was not right. I didn't need it for writing. I had to get rid of it.

· · ·

In art we made Advent wreaths of construction paper, green foam and pink, white and purple candles. I could do homework without my left hand but I couldn't cut leaves out of green construction paper without it. I felt dizzy and teary using that hand. I thought I could smell smoke and sweat on it. When I took a deep breath and looked up, wanting to look out the window because sometimes looking at the sky helped, Miss Boudreaux gave me the funniest look. I wiped my cheeks in case I was crying without knowing it; sometimes Yolanda had to wipe my face before we walked into school or I'd notice dozens of drops on my shirt that I hadn't felt fall.

• • •

I dreamed Mamalita pushed the house away, flew me to the park and sat me on a swing. She pushed me hard and I rose into the sky, sweeping over trees, the cool mist of clouds on my skin. Her voice in my ear said it was time to stop crying, to save my tears for later, when I needed them. I woke and wanted to cry because I knew she was gone but I swallowed until the sharp lump in my throat was only a pebble.

• • •

We spent the last few days before Christmas vacation making tree ornaments and helping kindergartners and first graders practice the songs they would sing in the school's Christmas Mass on Friday. The sixth grade would sing, too, but I just mouthed the words. I hadn't raised my hand in Mr. Albert's class since Shirleen beat me for being "a slut," whatever she meant by that. I found that I couldn't talk sometimes, especially in Mr. Albert's class or if someone other than Yolanda looked at me. And when I saw Shirleen, I felt cold inside, like an abandoned building.

The poinsettias and green wreaths were pretty against the gold trim of the altar. During Mass, I tried to stand still, look straight ahead at the poinsettias on the altar and near the doors, ignore the sharp sweat smell that seemed to be in the flesh of my nose, and when a hand touched my arm, I squealed. It was Sister Lawrence. She took my hand and led me outside.

It was a damp gray day, cool like inside the church but I could breathe outside. Sister Lawrence held my hand while I took a few deep breaths then cried a little. She gave me tissues from her habit pocket.

"Sandrine," she said. I was surprised to hear her say my name and looked at her face. "I'm so sorry." She hugged me. She smelled like church incense. I cried again, harder. She rubbed my back until I stopped sobbing then found more tissues. After I cleaned myself, I tried to dry the wet spots I'd made on her brown habit. "Don't worry, I have another one," she said with a gentle laugh. Her face became serious. "Are you ready to go back in?" Sister Lawrence held my shoulders and bent down to look in my eyes. "I'll go with you, Sandrine," she said. "I know it's hard without your grandmother. Every Christmas and Easter Mass, all I can think about is my—" I hadn't remembered Mamalita and I felt so ashamed, I busted out crying again, blind with tears, gasping for breath with my nose plugged tight. I held on to her habit, clenched it in my right hand, the left behind my back. Sister Lawrence touched the top of my head then reached behind me and grabbed my left hand. I jumped and tried to pull it away from her, it was just too dirty, too dirty.

"There isn't a speck of dust on your hand, Sandrine," Sister Lawrence said. "What do you mean?"

I heard what sounded like a thick old voice but slowly recognized it as mine, full of tears, hoarse, broken by hiccup sobs, and Sister Lawrence's hand slowly held both my hands tighter and tighter. When I stopped, she dabbed at my cheeks and eyes and I wanted to cry more because the hand so gentle, the tissue so soft, made me think of Mamalita.

Sister Lawrence held up more tissues while I blew and blew. I was able to breathe a little out of each nostril but I could only smell my own mucus and tears. " . . . and he made me lose the rosary I made," I said, remembering the rosary for the first time and wanting to cry all over again. I would never, I knew, feel that sunlight pride of Mamalita again.

"You said your mother saw him? Did she say anything to him?"

"She said I'm a slut."

Sister Lawrence held me tight against her and I felt what I thought were kisses on top of my head. She leaned me away and looked right in my face. I felt like no one had ever looked in my face before. Her nose was red, her eyes a little pink like she was about to cry herself. I had made her sad. "I'm sorry ..."

"You did not a single thing wrong. Let's go back in."

"I can't," I said, full of tears again.

"Oh, Sandrine, my poor little girl." She bent down again and took my face in her hands. "If that sinner of sinners Mary of Egypt can worship in God's house, you who have committed no sin certainly can ... You need God and Jesus and especially our mother Mary right now."

She held my hand just tight enough and we walked in together. We had missed communion, I was glad of that, and we spent the rest of the Mass in a small pew near the side door. Yolanda looked around with a worried frown until she saw me then her face broke into a big smile and she waved. Sister Mary Clare tapped her head with a bony finger. Sister Lawrence held my hand tightly as all the kids walked out in two rows then she told me to wait in the pew. She said something to an altar boy who brought Father MacNeeley out the sacristy. He nodded at her and she waved me over. We knelt close together and Father MacNeeley gave us communion. Sister Lawrence herself took me back to my classroom and I felt wrung out, damp and fuzzy-headed, like part of my insides were gone and I'd lost density.

The hour of school after Mass, the sixth-graders helped the second-graders finish aluminum foil ornaments and stars. I sat with Yolanda and made a star, too.

"Do you wish Philipa would call you or come for you as your Christmas present?" I said.

"No," Yolanda said.

I hadn't heard anything from Dad. Part of me hoped to see

him on the porch Christmas Day with presents but I knew that if he hadn't called or written yet, he wouldn't. But I was starting to agree with what I overheard Shirleen say on the phone—how could he want a woman who threw away her own daughter?

I went back to my classroom for my books and waited for Yolanda in the front doorway. We had almost reached Broad when I heard my name called. Sister Lawrence ran to us, holding up something small and red in one hand, her habit billowing in the cool damp breeze. She had a huge smile on her face as she put the small leather case in my hand. "Merry Christmas," she said and ran back into school. The case had a single snap. I opened it. Inside was a rosary made of blue and white glass beads with a wood medallion and a crucifix. The crucifix looked soft and smooth, a shade lighter in front than in back, like it had been rubbed. It smelled like roses.

"The nuns kiss theirs, don't they?" Yolanda said.

I didn't have a pocket in my jacket so I just held it. At Broad, Yolanda turned the wrong way. "This way, Yolanda."

She grinned and opened her hand. She had a five dollar bill and change. "Let's go get some ice cream."

"Where'd you get the money?"

"Do you want ice cream?"

I thought about it while the light changed from green to yellow to red. "Okay," I said.

• • •

Joe Henry came for dinner. I couldn't remember a friend of Shirleen's sitting at the table with us for dinner; they came to parties, they came after dinner and Shirleen might give them a plate of cold leftovers, but not at the table with us, like a part of the family or a father. I had seen Champ's car parked near the schoolyard but he was gone by dismissal and we hadn't seen him around the house since he trapped me in the yard. Though I'd liked Joe Henry before, him at the table turned my stomach and I couldn't eat. Shirleen told me to eat or she'd make me but Joe Henry said I might be coming down with the flu and his hand reaching out to check my forehead for fever made what felt like a quickly inflating balloon of screams fill my chest so much my back started to hurt and then I was on the floor, on my back, still sitting in the chair. I got up, set the chair back and went to the bathroom, Shirleen saying, "She's just bent out of shape 'cause I beat her ass for being fresh, that's all . . . I know what I saw."

I wanted to cry but my chest and back hurt too much. I sat on the edge of the tub. There was a soft knock at the door then Joe Henry popped his head in. I started shaking.

"You all right?" His forehead was wrinkled up like he was worried and I wanted to tell him everything but if I did, I'd get another beating from Shirleen, I was sure.

Joe Henry opened the door a little then looked at me again and stayed still. "You sure you feel all right?" he said. I thought someone else was crying until I realized I had busted out in loud sobs that almost rolled me off the edge of the tub.

"Shut up in there," Shirleen said. "Whatever she tells you is a lie."

Joe Henry shook his head and closed the door. "I think she got the flu," he said.

• • •

We window-shopped with Shirleen on Canal Street, each with lists we could put five things on. Yolanda was so excited it was almost Christmas she didn't believe Shirleen would only get one thing we wanted and one thing we needed. After the stores, Yolanda wrote her list over and over, trying to get the most wanted things at the top of the list. Her list was all toys.

I wanted a school sweater with pockets, a purse, some books. Shirleen's eyebrows went up when she read my list but she didn't say anything. She grinned at Yolanda's. And on Christmas day, Yolanda got one Barbie, two workbooks, and a sweater to match her uniform. She circled the little tree we had crammed between the sofa and wall, sure more toys were hidden. "Books?" she said. "Books?" I didn't get books but I did get a new sweater and a purse; inside the purse was a five dollar bill and a compact mirror. We spent the rest of the day at Mother Dear's, the house full of aunts, uncles, cousins, friends of Mother Dear's, neighbors bringing little gifts and food. I expected to see Champ and felt all day like I couldn't breathe. Putting my paper plate in the garbage bag tied to the back door, I looked up and saw his face and funny-colored eyes. I wanted to shrink down into the crowd but he saw me, winked and made kisses in my direction.

Yolanda played with the kids. I watched them. I felt sick to my stomach inside the house, the crowd in the kitchen, squeezing through tall loud bodies to get to the bathroom made my skin feel like it didn't fit. I didn't watch the kids as much as I looked in their direction without seeing them, just feeling sunlight on my face and wishing I could have stayed in bed, just that one day.

$$\bullet \quad \bullet \quad \bullet$$

On my birthday I asked Shirleen to show me how to do my hair different ways instead of the two braids I'd been wearing since kindergarten. In the bathroom with the other girls at recess, my hair in two buns at the back of my head, I thought I finally looked like I would grow up, almost the same height as the others, my face just a little rounder.

Sister Michael watched the boys on the other side of the yard, the bigger side near the trees, while the eighth-grade girl chosen to watch recess for that month sat on a bench on the smaller side for the girls, near the walkway to the cafeteria and the gate facing the street and church. Her wide face was light brown, her hair thick and straight, a big smile with perfect teeth, dark round eyes. She wasn't black but I didn't think she was exactly white either. Four sixth-grade girls crowded on the bench next to her—a group always sat near the eighth-grade girl, trying to look important or older. She spoke to them just a little, then opened her purse and took out a jar. In the jar were thin round pads she wiped her nose and forehead with. I wanted to be closer, to see what else was in her purse. I hadn't started bringing mine to school yet because I didn't want just a rosary and mirror inside; I needed to know what other girls had in theirs first. Later they told me her name. Lydia.

After school, Yolanda came with me to the K&B. A sign on the front door said the soda fountain would close at the end of the month. "Oh, no!" Yolanda said. She followed me through the store, counting her change. I didn't need a jar like Lydia, or Stridex pads to wipe off oil I didn't have yet, but I found a comb and brush that fit in my purse and bought hairpins so I wouldn't have to use Shirleen's.

• • •

Yolanda stayed after school twice a week to do extra work with Sister Lawrence. I waited in the doorway of the school for the seventh and eighth grade girls to leave school. Lydia stood right next to me for almost five minutes talking to another girl. She couldn't find something in her purse and set it on the step near me to dig through it. I heard rattling and clinking, saw the Stridex jar, mirror, comb, brush, flowered coin purse, key ring, candy, and what she was looking for—a red address book. She wrote down the girl's number and they walked off together. While they walked, Lydia twisted up her long hair and wrapped a rubber band around it.

Yolanda came out and we walked home. She kept talking to me, looking into my face when I didn't answer. She gave up the last few blocks and hugged her books to her chest. I couldn't think how to get Lydia to talk to me. I didn't want to watch from the side of the yard while she sat near the other sixth-grade girls. I wanted to know what her hair smelled like.

I had been in seventh-grade math most of the school year but only now noticed some eighth-grade girls were in the class then, too, but not Lydia. I wore my hair a different way every day until I ran out of ideas. Shirleen had no more ideas or didn't want to tell. She looked at me like she thought I was doing something behind her back. When she said Yolanda should walk herself home when she stayed after school, Yolanda begged harder and longer than she had to for me to keep walking with her then smiled at me like she'd won me a prize.

• • •

I heard Shirleen talking in the dark as I went from the bathroom to the bedroom. I looked in the bedroom and Yolanda seemed already asleep so I stood as still as I could in the doorway, one ear turned to Shirleen. She didn't have the light or TV on and I could just see the top of her head against the front window, pale green from the streetlight. I saw bits of bouncing light, the spiral phone cord bouncing up and down as she talked.

"The hard thing is to tell her the mistake without encouraging her to make it," Shirleen said. "Well . . . Like I'm proud to be a typist making $7000 a year? And with two mouths to feed now? . . . Girl, they ain't coming for her, would you? . . . That's what I thought." She was quiet a long time. "I know what I saw . . . No, I cannot be wrong, I saw him and I saw her . . . Yeah."

She laughed big and loud and threw back her head so I could see light outlining her open mouth and teeth. "Shouldn't I be?" She listened awhile. My chest hurt from holding my breath. Suddenly she slammed the phone down and sucked her teeth. I stepped back into my room. Mother Dear and Auntie Z had told me about Shirleen and Dad, how he met her at a free clinic. Mother Dear said they never got married and I was a bastard but Auntie Z told me to pay no mind to Dear's mean talk because most of it wasn't true though Auntie Z didn't tell me which was true and which was mean lying talk. Uncle Frank and Uncle Jerry wouldn't even say my dad's name. Sometimes I thought Shirleen hated me because I looked like Dad, skin color-wise at least, but now she hated me because she thought I was like her and would get pregnant before I finished high school, like her and Dear. My stomach jumped and bubbled thinking she thought I liked Champ, liked him pushing my hand in his pants or his scratchy fingers on my panties.

• • •

Sister Lawrence gave me palm-sized books of life stories of women saints and I read them at recess so I didn't have to watch the other girls sitting so close to Lydia. I walked back and forth in the covered walkway between the school and cafeteria, reading the one-page stories, glancing at Lydia combing her hair, slipping something from her purse into her mouth and chewing or sucking quietly or smiling weakly at one of the girls. When we lined up to go back to class, I smelled candy near me. Lydia. She touched the book in my hands. "What is that?" she said. She turned the book so she could see. "Oh. I wondered what you were reading over there." And she walked away, up the stairs ahead of us to her class on the third floor, her thick braid swinging back and forth, the curled end brushing her lower back.

. . .

Sister Michael let Lydia keep watching the girls' side of the yard but made the girls who sat by Lydia walk around, saying they sat all day and should exercise. I walked back and forth pretending to read my book of saints. Lydia folded her legs under her and ignored the girls walking around the yard together in a group.

I asked permission to go inside to the water fountain. She said, "Uh-huh." When I came out, I sat on the bench. Lydia combed a section of her hair and started braiding it. "Can you cornrow your hair?" she said.

I had to swallow to get my voice back. "My grandmother used to all the time. My mother, never. She says it looks ghetto."

Lydia smiled. "My mother hates braids. She says I look like a wetback." She finished the braid and tied the hair in a knot to keep it from unraveling. Her hair was shiny and pure black and completely straight. No amount of hot combing or oil or brushing could make my hair that straight or shiny. "You're in seventh-grade math, right?"

"Yeah."

"It's not fair and you should be really mad. Sandrine, right?"

"Yeah." I felt a sweet tremble in my chest. "What's not fair?"

"You don't—the honor roll. If you're in seventh-grade math, your grades must be the highest in sixth grade but he," she pointed to the other side of the yard and I didn't know who she meant, "is on the Alpha roll instead of you. All 'cause you're a girl. I know. They did it to me, too. I didn't get to be on the Alpha roll until seventh, when there were no boys to put ahead of me. I'm glad I'm not going to a coed school after this." I thought for a while then knew who she meant, David Casimir, who got lots of As but Bs in math and geography. And he had been on the

Alpha roll since second grade. I could never figure out why with straight As, except for Father MacNeeley's C, I was on the Beta roll every semester and, thinking about the list on the wall by the principal's office, why the Alpha roll was always all boys.

"It's not fair."

"You're right!" she said. "'Cause you're a girl. You know what Sister Mary Joseph said to me? 'Books don't find husbands.' Like I want one. They're disgusting."

"My parents divorced."

"Really? Wow." There were kids whose fathers had died and mothers remarried but few had divorced parents; the nuns never talked about it. "So it's just you and your mom?"

"And Yolanda."

"Oh, wow, all girls, that must be so great. I wish. I got four brothers, a doormat of a mother and the Pig." She smiled. The bell rang. "Since you can't be first in honor roll, you be first in line," she said with a big smile. She had a dimple in her right cheek and though I'd never paid much attention to Yolanda's dimples, I thought Lydia's made her beautiful. I could hardly focus on school the rest of the day because she'd talked to me.

Yolanda and I left school on time that day but I knew the next day she'd be working with Sister Lawrence. At the K&B, while Yolanda had a root beer float at the soda fountain for the last time, I bought a small manicure set, and a compact of face powder like I'd seen in Lydia's purse but the pale shade, not the light brown I was sure she had. She used it on her nose to dull the oily shine; I just wanted to know what it smelled like. I also bought a yellow diary with a lock, and a pen with ink that smelled like bubble gum. I wrote on the first fresh white page while Yolanda brushed her teeth before bed. I tried to write down every word I remembered Lydia saying and had just written, "mother and me and the Pig" when Yolanda walked in smelling like Pepsodent and tried to look over my shoulder. I pressed the open diary to my chest and she looked hurt.

"What are you writing?" she said.

"None of your business."

"Why?"

I went to the bathroom to finish.

• • •

I finished the last question in the last chapter of the social studies book. I knew from fifth grade that we would probably not finish the book but I had all the homework answers ready in a folder at home. I heard a car motor; my heart jumped and I had to catch my breath but I kept my head down, looking instead at the signatures on the inside front cover, seven who had used the book before and I knew none had ever read the whole thing and answered all the questions. I wanted to feel proud of myself but I still felt like an abandoned house, empty, cold, musty.

The motor faded for a minute then came back and stopped in front of me. I looked up, hoping it was a mother come late or someone looking at the school for next year; already several parents had walked through our classroom or peeked in the windows. But the car was red. My leg muscles trembled, I wanted to get up and run but the third floor bell rang and I knew he'd be distracted by the older girls. I scooted until I was deeper in the doorway, skirt wrapped tight around my legs.

Lydia didn't come out with the other girls. After they had scattered, the red car was still there, engine purring, and I took a quick look. Champ smiled and winked at me, waved his hand then, when I didn't move, crooked his finger at me to come closer. "Hey, yella gal, come here, come on over here." Then he laughed. "I been missing you. How Yolanda doing? Tell your mama I'm-a come by Friday night, see all my girls."

I felt sick. I took the rosary out of my purse and held it tight in my hand. The beads and grooves of the crucifix and medal dug into my skin and I started to feel better.

"Hey."

Lydia. "Hi," I said.

She looked worried and knelt down next to me. "Are you okay?" Her eyes were wide and waiting. I swallowed. Lydia touched my shoulder. She shook her head then folded her arms around me. Her hair smelled candy-sweet. I felt my body shaking.

"That's sweet you got a new friend." His voice. I tensed and Lydia tensed with me.

"Are you looking for somebody?" Lydia said.

"Only you, baby."

I felt Lydia fumble in her purse then jerk her body. I heard a loud thunk, like something hitting the car, then a quiet dull crack. I peeked around Lydia and saw Champ, eyes narrowed, pointing at us as his car slid away. Lydia's Stridex jar lay leaking in the street.

"Pervert bastard," Lydia said. My eyes teared up and Lydia jerked a tissue out her purse. "Tell me later, you don't have to tell me now, okay?"

Yolanda skipped out. She looked confused when Lydia started to walk with us. Lydia showed me how to hold keys in my hand with the points sticking out, a sharp fist to scratch, poke or punch with. I told her the back ways we took to school and she said I was smart, that she hadn't thought of it. She asked me to show her the streets we used another time. Her house on Broad St., a small white shotgun with rooms added to the back and side so it was shaped like a T, was only five blocks from our street. The yard was bigger than the house, grass perfectly cut, a blue and white Mary statue in the middle of the yard, the pedestal surrounded by knee-high rosebushes. When Lydia opened the door to go in, we heard noise, like a TV turned up too loud.

• • •

I sniffed my uniform for Lydia's sweet smell before I hung it up for the next day and helped Yolanda with her homework and workbooks; we only had time for chores on the weekend and never at Mother Dear's anymore.

Yolanda finished the last worksheet as Shirleen came in the front door. Dishes were still in the sink, the floors were gritty, and the beds were unmade. Shirleen walked through the house then came back to the kitchen table. "This just will not do, not anymore," she said. She put her purse down on my textbooks. "Either you finish her work sooner or you do your homework later because this place is filthy."

I ignored her, pushed her purse off and opened my English book. Shirleen slammed the book closed. "I was talking to you, not myself," she said.

"Yolanda is done and she can do it."

"I said I was talking to you so get up and get this place in order." She went to the living room. Yolanda's eyes got big as I opened my book again. Yolanda heard Shirleen's footsteps, ran to the sink and started running water and moving dishes. Shirleen came in. "What did I tell you?" she said to me.

I looked at her. "I spent two hours helping Yolanda and now I am going to do my own homework."

"I told you—"

"I am not failing sixth grade because she's stupid and you're lazy."

"Lazy? Lazy!" She flapped her arms. I couldn't not smile. "I work all damn day and I'm lazy? I pay the bills, I keep both of you in food and uniforms and allowance—"

"Who gets an allowance?" I said. Yolanda turned away.

"I'm the only one working here and I'm lazy? When I was your age, little Miss Privilege, I cooked, cleaned and helped five kids with homework every damn day and still did my homework and—"

"You give Yolanda an allowance and not me?"

Shirleen froze. "To get better grades."

"I haven't gotten an allowance since school ended last year."

"Really?" Shirleen said. "Oh."

I picked up my books and went to the bedroom. I pushed the dresser toward the door but Shirleen opened the door a little before I got the dresser flat against it.

"Open this door!"

"No!" I couldn't believe she was so adamant about me not doing my homework. Other kids got yelled at because they didn't do their homework. Shirleen pounded and kicked at the door and I knew that she wanted to get in and beat me with Sock It to Me. I spread my books on the bed and it was hard to concentrate but I started reading. By the time I'd read half my English assignment, Shirleen was gone and I had quiet. After homework, I didn't go to the bathroom, just put on my pajamas and got into bed. It felt good to stretch out my arms and legs, to have the bed to myself. I wrote in the diary about the walk home with Lydia. I put the diary down then thought to write what had happened over homework. As I wrote, it felt like I was writing Mamalita another letter she wouldn't get, and after I wrote I was angrier at Shirleen than I had been when she pounded on the door.

• • •

"My stepfather says educating a girl is a waste," Lydia said with a sour face. I made a sour face, too. I couldn't imagine my dad saying anything like that but he had been gone with Philipa so long I couldn't say I knew him anymore. "I'm applying to Dominican, I don't care what he says. I'll get a scholarship, I don't care what I have to do, I'll clean the nun's toilets, I'll . . ." She started playing with her hair then divided it to braid it. "What school do you want to go to?"

"Dominican."

"Good for you. Don't let them stop you. At least there are no men in your house to shit on your dreams."

I looked around to see if any sisters heard. Sister Michael was on the boys' side of the yard, holding two boys apart and yelling.

"And you should make Yolanda do her own work," Lydia said. As soon as I'd sat next to her on the bench, I had told her about Shirleen. "You have to keep your grades high to get a scholarship. And you'll have a good chance 'cause David will be gone next year and you'll be on the Alpha roll. Schools pay a lot of attention to things like that," she said with a big warm smile. She stopped braiding her hair. "Tomorrow, tomorrow I'll show you some things to do with your hair." I grinned back and she hugged me. "You're better than any of the girls in my class, even. You and me know things about the world, about the evil of people, of men. None of them," she waved her hand at the girls standing in the covered walkway, "know what we know."

• • •

I spread out Yolanda's homework and worksheets and took my books to the bedroom. Before I'd finished reading the first column of "The Fall of the House of Usher," I heard the TV. "I'll tell," I said. When it got dark, my stomach flipped and flopped; Shirleen would be home soon. I'd finished most of my homework when I heard the TV click off then the door unlock and open. "Finished already?" she said to Yolanda. Shirleen didn't notice me when she walked by my door to the kitchen. "Oh, good the . . . Sandi!"

I expected stupidity and ignorant insult from Yolanda but I wanted to hit something every time I heard Shirleen use that name. I leaned closer to the book and breathed deep and hard, wishing I could snort fire on Shirleen and Yolanda and Champ and—

"Sandi! Sandi!"

"I'm doing my homework."

Shirleen stood in my doorway. "I don't care if you got an audience with the Pope, you come when I call, you hear!"

"I'm doing my homework."

"Yolanda did not finish her work."

"I told her to. She watched TV—"

"I told you to make sure she did it, I told you she is your responsibility after school and if she doesn't finish, you pay the price."

"That's ridiculous. I get straight A's and I am not going to fall behind because Dummy won't do her homework!" I said.

Shirleen stomped into my room with Sock It to Me. I wielded my English book and when she got close enough, I knocked the paddle out of her hand. I heard water running in the kitchen—Yolanda starting dishes. Shirleen reached for the paddle and I kicked it under my bed. She came at me with both hands in the air, ready to strike. "If you make me fail I will hate you forever, I will never, never forgive you, never!" She stopped, breathing hard, her mouth so tight the lips were black and puckered. She got on her knees to get the Sock It to Me from under the bed. I felt like she was trying to erase me and put Yolanda in my place. She hadn't checked the TV to see if it was warm from three hours of watching, she didn't do dishes even if I had a test, if Yolanda forgot to put one of her uniform skirts in the laundry Shirleen blamed me and gave Yolanda one of mine to wear, to punish me because Yolanda forgot. I didn't understand why she hated me so or at least why she favored Yolanda so much when she didn't want her here in the first place. Her head was close to my feet and I wanted to kick it.

She noticed me looking at her. Maybe she saw what I was feeling because she backed away and left without the paddle. And even closed my door. I heard the water and splashing in the kitchen stop. A chair scraped on the floor. I opened the book but I couldn't focus on the words. I took my diary out of my purse, wrote the date then "Dear Lydia" and wrote. Afterwards, I copied the best parts on a sheet of paper and folded it into a tight packet like I saw the other sixth-grade girls do when they passed notes in class, wrote Lydia's name on both sides and tucked it in my purse.

Yolanda came to bed when I was almost asleep. She laid down heavily. "Now I don't get my allowance anymore," she said.

"And I'm supposed to feel sorry for you?" I said. She turned away from me and I sat up so she could hear me. "You turn my mother against me because I want to do my homework? You get an allowance for barely getting Cs, Cs you get because I make you work?" I jerked myself down and folded my arms. "You and me are through."

"What?"

I didn't answer. She said, "Sandi?" turned toward me, apologized. I didn't look at her. I turned to the wall and made sure there was empty space between us in bed. I thought about Lydia, how to get the note to her before recess, and decided, to hell with Yolanda, I was walking home with Lydia every day.

• • •

Lydia was quiet. She spent a long time brushing her hair smooth, starting braids, changing her mind, undoing them, starting again. I slipped my note into her purse. When she went into it for a rubber band, she saw the note and smiled at me, almost her usual smile. Then, looking around first, she put a tightly folded note into my purse.

"Let me fix your hair," she said.

I had made a single braid and wrapped it into a bun at the back of my head. I turned to face the church and felt Lydia taking out hairpins. "You use a lot of hairpins," she said.

"It comes apart if I don't."

"You need some hair spray." She undid the braid and started to make several little braids which she curled and pinned to my head; I imagined my hair would look like a highway cloverleaf. "What happened," she said, "what'd that man do?" I took a deep shaky breath. Lydia put her hands on my shoulder and whispered, "I'll never tell, Sister Michael is way over there, and you know I'd kick him in the face for you . . . You can tell me."

"He . . . followed us a lot. Then he was at our house, I think he was hiding and then he was all over the alley and I couldn't get out." I wiped sweat off my face though it was a cool day and everyone wore sweaters.

"That's not all, is it?"

I felt strange inside, shaky because I was telling it again but also another feeling was in there, something that felt lighter, a space where I could breathe. "He opened his pants. And he put my hand in there. He pushed me in the backyard and he, he had my panties down when Shirleen came home and then she beat the shit out of me."

"Bitch! She thought, what? That you wanted him to follow you home?" I looked down at my lap and shrugged though a little bit of me wanted to smile when Lydia called Shirleen a bitch. "Just a goddamn bitch . . . ."

She pinned the last small braid and I felt them with my fingers. They were smooth; I couldn't feel any of the pins, not like when I did my hair. My chest hurt feeling Lydia's kindness and Shirleen's hatred at the same time.

Sister Michael rang the big hand bell. Lydia lined up the girls while Sister Michael lined up the boys. I held my purse, and Lydia's note, tight to my side.

We walked Lydia home in silence, Lydia and I close to each other, our skirts touching, our arms rubbing a few times. She opened her gate and said, "You are right and Shirleen is wrong." I smiled; she'd read my note. She took her time unlocking the door, like she didn't want to go in. Then she lifted her head, shook her braids and stepped inside.

Yolanda walked almost a block ahead while I read Lydia's note. The Pig, she wrote, "put his dirty cock in my mouth and made me swallow, AGAIN." I tasted sour milk laced with pungent salt and felt my stomach heave. I swallowed hard and read the note again to make sure I'd read it right. She and I did know things.

• • •

Seventh and eighth grades had early dismissal, at the same time as the rest of us, and we walked home with Lydia and her brothers, the boys behind us balancing on curbs then running ahead and doubling back, throwing a baseball over our heads so close I could feel it brush stray hairs. Lydia yelled at them but they either didn't turn around or just stuck out their tongues or pretended to fart on us.

"I'm-a tell Mommy you walked with that nigger girl," the skinniest said; he had messy red-brown hair and smelled like he never washed.

Lydia's face twisted up and I had a flash of Philipa looming over me. "You little piece of white trash shit!" Lydia yelled at him. When she dropped her books and purse and took off running after him, I shoved my books and purse at Yolanda and ran, too. All four boys ran the block to their yard, three scattering to the back of the yard as Lydia caught the skinny red-brown haired one by the back of the head and threw him down to the grass. I caught up as she sat on him, drawing her arms back behind her and slapping and punching his head, neck and back. He tried to reach behind to grab her and clung onto her skirt. I kicked his hand off and held his arms down while Lydia landed one final punch to his back, each shoulder and his head, jamming his face deep in the grass. Then she made a sick sound in her throat, lifted up enough to roll him over and spit right between his eyes. The other three boys laughed and cheered but when Lydia stood, eyes narrow and hot, they disappeared behind the house.

"I'm-a—"

"Fuck you," Lydia said, bending down into his face. He opened his mouth, glanced quickly at me than ran behind the house with his brothers.

Yolanda stood at the open gate, holding all the books, the purses around her neck. "Thanks," I said as I took all but her second-grade books. "Now go home."

"But . . ."

I turned away from her.

"Wait here," Lydia said. The boys were in the yard, throwing the baseball around the Virgin Mary statue. Lydia went inside for a minute then came back to the door with a big smile. "Come on in," she said.

It was dark and quiet. I thought someone was sitting on the sofa but as we passed, I saw it was just piles of clothes; there was a pile in the easy chair next to the TV, too. I didn't tell Lydia it was the first time I'd been in a white house. I sniffed deep to see if it smelled different and it did, no undercurrents of garlic or onions, more a smell of boiled meat. I folded my arms, too, afraid to touch anything, and also nervous because if I left our house the way Lydia's looked, even if Shirleen didn't work all day, I'd be bright pink all over from Sock It to Me. I followed Lydia past one darkened bedroom, the double bed half-made, another bedroom with two sets of bare double mattresses on the floor and the rest of the floor space covered by toys, balls, paper airplanes, boys' clothes and shoes. At the end of the hall were the two rooms that made the T of the shotgun—to the right a big blue, white and green kitchen, some bowls from breakfast still on the table, on the left a closed door. The yellow ribbon around Lydia's neck, which I'd always thought was a scapular, had instead of a plastic medal of Mary a key she used to unlock her bedroom door.

Her room was neat and small, the curtains open to let in lots of sunlight. I'd never liked the color yellow much but her butterscotch-colored walls made me want a yellow room. The wood floor was clean and shiny like the top of her desk and the white headboard of her twin bed. We could hear the boys yelling outside.

"I'm not supposed to walk with you anymore," she said. She looked at herself in the mirror on the wall by the closet door, smoothed her hair. "Mom said because you're younger than me but the Pig says I should stick with my 'own' kind. To hell with him. If I did that, I wouldn't be around any of them, that's for sure.

"Do you know how to play solitaire?" she said. "Let's play double solitaire." She dealt out the cards and we sat cross-legged on the floor by the closet, where the light shone in but not in our eyes or on our skin. Lydia had just shuffled and dealt out another round when her head snapped up to the clock.

"You have to go," she said, eyes big. She checked the hall before we tiptoed through the kitchen, out the kitchen door and driveway gate to the sidewalk. Lydia looked over her shoulder then went into the house without saying goodbye.

• • •

When we turned the corner onto our street, Yolanda started running to the house. A big green car was parked in front. Philipa's car. Good, I thought. Now Lydia could keep me company after school. I hadn't talked to Yolanda since that morning when I told her to hurry up or we'd be late for school. She had looked scared and lonely. It annoyed me.

She stood on the top stair with her hands behind her back. And the man in the chair was Dad. He stood, took one of Yolanda's hands and put a piece of paper in it. Yolanda heard my footsteps and moved out of the way. I didn't want to hug him but I did and I had missed him and he squeezed me tight, a warm Dad hug.

I noticed Yolanda standing near us. "Go inside and do your homework," I said to her. "She's failing everything," I said to Dad.

"I am not!" Yolanda said and ran inside.

"Good," I said.

"Cream pie," Dad said.

"If she doesn't do her homework, Shirleen whips me. I stopped getting an allowance and Shirleen gives it to her for getting D's while I'm getting all A's even though I spend more time on Yolanda's homework than mine." I wanted to spit because I was angry at Yolanda, the Pig, Shirleen. Then I wanted to cry because I knew Dad wasn't taking me anywhere. Philipa could be waiting for him. I just wanted them to take Yolanda so I could be with Lydia, get my allowance back, have less to fight with Shirleen about.

"Yolanda's not as smart as you," he said in a quiet voice.

"How would she know? She watches TV all the time. And I tell Shirleen and she acts like I'm lying . . . "

"Shirleen?" He had a little smile. "You two must really be butting heads for you to call her Shirleen. I don't think I even called her Shirleen." He smiled. When I didn't smile his brow wrinkled and he rubbed my back. "Can I do anything?"

I thought, You can kick Shirleen's ass then kick the Pig's ass, but I just shook my head. He offered to take me, and only me, to McDonald's. After we got into Philipa's big car, he said he had to go back to Jackson that night. Work, he said.

While I was eating my Big Mac I asked if Philipa was waiting, if Yolanda needed to pack. I was hoping. I didn't feel sorry for her anymore. She'd taken too much of mine.

"Well, no," Dad said.

"No?"

"Well . . . " He finished his shake in one big suck. "I finally left my crazy wife."

"Your second crazy wife."

He laughed then tried to make his face serious. "You shouldn't talk about your mother that way. She loves you and takes good care of you. Most of the time," he said with a little smile. "My car broke down one day and I took Phil's. I came home from work the next day and it was gone. She sold it to somebody and wouldn't tell me who so I took her car and left." He offered me his French fries. "She didn't even talk about Yolanda. I thought it was a visit, I really did. But once Yolanda was gone, she never mentioned her. I told her she should call and she looked at me like she didn't know who I was talking about. Shit, I don't want to talk about her." I loved him. I loved him and I loved Lydia.

"Do you wonder what you were thinking?"

Dad leaned on the table and looked in my eyes, maybe trying to see who I was. He smiled. "Finish up so you can get to your homework."

"I'm gonna get a scholarship for high school," I said.

He reached over and squeezed my hand. It felt good.

It was dark when we left the McDonald's. I felt full and happy. When he stopped the car across Mother Dear's empty driveway, he took some paper out of his back pocket and unfolded it. "I need to know," he said in a quiet voice, "if this is true or you were, I don't know, angry or upset." He held the pages out to me. I saw my lopsided scrawl on the folded pages. My letter to Mamalita. The fullness in my stomach soured and I felt a little dizzy. I thought of Lydia's note, "dirty cock" and "swallow"; swallow what?

"Yes."

"Okay," he said in a whisper, to me or himself, I wasn't sure. "Look in the glove compartment. For a pen," he said as he reached in his back pocket again. I found a pen and gave it to him. I looked at the lit windows of the house. I would go straight to my room to do my homework. I was glad I didn't have to eat with Shirleen and Yolanda. Dad gave me the letter with his address and phone number written on the back of the last page. "You call me, you write me," he said. "When I get time off, I'll come see you, okay?"

"Okay." My eyes were wet. I had forgotten he was nice.

"And here. Don't let Shirleen see. Just for you, not her, not Yolanda, understand?" And he gave me a roll of money, thick like a sausage, bound with a green rubber band. I tucked it in my purse right away and found myself hugging him tight. I didn't want him to go but knew he had to and would. I was glad he'd taken Philipa's car. And I was glad he'd come to see me.

After a few kisses back and forth, I got out of the car and watched him drive away. I felt sad and happy but when I unlocked the front door, all my anger came back. I went straight to the bathroom to look in my purse. The roll of bills was all fives, tens and twenties, with a hundred dollar bill in the middle. I swooned on the side of the tub where I sat. It was too much to even think of spending. I wondered if it was enough for four years at Dominican.

I sat up in bed to pray my rosary. Yolanda watched me a while, surprised, then went to sleep. I prayed the rosary for Lydia. I didn't pray anymore for myself or world peace or for all the hungry children in Africa, like Shirleen said to, and in church I said the words and stood and kneeled at all the right times without thinking about it, my mind on other things— math class, a wet lump of paper in my hands, fear in my muscles, scraping fingertips.

In the middle of a Hail Mary I remembered—Dad had given Yolanda something. I shook her shoulder until she woke up. "What did my dad give you?"

"Huh?"

I tried to sound like Shirleen. "What did he give you?"

"A piece of paper," she said, turning her face into her pillow.

"What was on it?" She took a deep breath but didn't answer. "Philipa's address? Huh? Huh?" She didn't move. "When I find it, and I will find it, I will call her and you will go home. Let her help you with your homework, let her walk you home from school. You know she won't. She'll leave you in the house all day and you'll forget what little you know now."

Yolanda jumped out of bed and ran out of the room. I stretched across the bed. And as I fell asleep I wondered why Champ had grabbed me instead of Yolanda. In my dream, the alley smelled like fried pork chops, a girl's arm tripped me and I fell on my back, Champ grinning and his thing, like a hairy hot sausage, dripping milk onto my bare legs.

The dream woke me. Yolanda had snuck back into bed, hugging the edge, taking as little space as she could.

. . .

Shirleen or Yolanda could go into any drawer at any time, the closet, too, and the roll was too thick to not be noticed under the mattress so I moved the money from hiding place to hiding place, at the same time looking for the paper Dad had given Yolanda. Then Shirleen threw away a tall narrow candy tin that still smelled of peppermints. I hid the tin in the bathroom before I took out the garbage, washed it in the tub during my bath and put the roll of money inside, watching the bills uncoil until they were snug.

In the morning I made Yolanda get ready early and sent her off to school alone. She turned to look at me every few steps and stopped at the corner of our street and Broad. I waved my arms and said, "Go on!" She hung her head and turned the corner.

I had to take a lot of deep breaths before I could go into the alley. I thought I could smell him. His face came to mind but closer than I'd ever seen it when he'd followed us; it seemed right above me, half-smiling, panting. I held the cold tin tight enough in my hand to chill and partly numb my hand, to make his face and smell fade enough for me to move. I crawled under the house, dug a hole with a rusted hand shovel and spent a long time smoothing the dirt over the tin so no one could see it.

I walked to school fast, brushing off my skirt and sweater. The skirt plaid was dark gray, white and red and my sweater dark gray so dirt wasn't too visible. I saw Yolanda far down Broad, waiting at the corner, like she couldn't cross the street without me. I stopped at Lydia's house.

I knocked on the door, got no answer and knocked harder and longer. I heard two people yell at each other in another language that I thought might be Spanish; I sometimes heard Sister Paul speaking it to the school janitor. The door flung open and Lydia's frown turned to a smile. "Hey. Wait right here," she said.

A man sat on the sofa, eating breakfast off a TV tray and watching TV. He wore a white undershirt and dark work pants. His salt-and-pepper hair and beard looked flat and dirty. And he was the same color as me; I thought he was white but the only light was the TV so I couldn't be sure. I guessed he was the Pig. Lydia's mother followed her to the porch. Her mom had the same flat wide face and light brown skin; her shiny black hair was cut short and she had rings around her eyes, like she didn't sleep. She looked me up and down then said to Lydia, "Do you have everything?"

"Uh-huh. Let's go." Lydia took my wrist and led me down the stairs and out of the yard. She didn't look back but I did and saw her mother standing by the fence, watching us.

"Thank God," Lydia said. "I couldn't wait for Monday." She started crying. I was so surprised I stood there awhile just looking at her. Then I thought to hug her; she was a little taller and she drooped over me to cry on my shoulder. I dug in my purse with one hand for tissues.

"Tell me," I said as we walked closer to Yolanda who still waited.

"Tell you what?"

"What he does. What it all means. I'm so sick of not understanding, not knowing what it all is, what he wanted to do to me, what that taste was . . ." We were a few feet from Yolanda but I stopped because I was ready to throw up. A car slowed down and a man inside stared at the three of us. I screamed and waved my fists at him and his car. "Go to hell!" I said. Lydia threw a handful of shells from a driveway and they peppered the car's bumper and back window. Then we all ran across the street to school.

. . .

Lydia dropped a note in my hand before she went into her house. It was thick, barely staying folded in its little packet. I set up to do my homework on the living room floor so Yolanda couldn't sneak away from her work in the kitchen to watch TV. My heart pounded, I was breathing fast, and my mouth went stale as I unfolded Lydia's note. It was three pages. The first page was graph paper; she'd drawn two profiles, one a naked man with a thing aimed up and an arrow pointing to it with some words for it written there—penis, cock, dick. The second profile was a naked woman with an open mouth and, instead of a second leg, Lydia had drawn a cross-section of the woman's insides below the waist. I leaned close and squinted because there seemed to be so many different things with lots of arrows and words. The next page started her note. "Here are the names for the evil you know. And you need to know what is inside of you so you can protect it." The penis, she said, was limp and small until something touched it or the man wanted to use it, then it sat up like a baton and that's when he could use it, in your mouth, in your vagina, in your anus. I felt like vomiting and stopped to breathe, the note folded closed so I could have a short break. The smell and face of Champ and Mister Tom's penis dripping milk lingered around me. And I learned that the pungent, salty taste in my vomit was what shot out of the penis. I felt like running but I wanted to know the rest. If they put it in your vagina, Lydia wrote, you could get pregnant. That's why the Pig had always put his in her mouth. Until last weekend.

It was dark outside. I hid the note in my purse, to finish the last page later. I stared at my homework but couldn't see individual words. My face hurt. I hurt more and more until from scalp to toes I went numb.

. . .

I left the note in my purse. I told Lydia I couldn't read it all at once. She nodded her head and hugged me with one arm.

Yolanda was at the kitchen table doing her homework. I looked through her books, between the mattresses, in all the drawers, under the bed, inside shoes. In the toe of her right tennis shoe I found a tightly folded piece of paper. I almost laughed out loud. On it was Philipa's name, the townhouse address, a new phone number and a work number.

. . .

A car slowed down to watch Yolanda, Lydia and I walk toward Lydia's house. The window was down and a man smiled at us. I picked up two big rocks, chunks of broken sidewalk, just in case.

"Go away!" I said.

"Man, you rude," he said, frowning at me.

"And you're a fucking pervert!" Lydia said. Yolanda stopped walking and covered her mouth as if she'd said it and Lydia laughed as loud as she could. The car drove away as slowly as it had approached us, the man in the passenger seat not smiling anymore but watching us hard with bright eyes.

Lydia's house was dim and quiet. She peeked in a bedroom, asked her mother if she could go to my house and we heard her mother say, "Yes," in a tired, weak voice. Lydia walked away rolling her eyes. "The Pig is still at work," she said loudly.

"Don't call him that," her mother said from the bedroom. "He's still your father."

"Stepfather," Lydia said. Lydia went back to the bedroom then came out a few seconds later with a half-smile, her mother yelling, "Liar! Liar!"

"I wonder if I should come back," Lydia said, still smirking. We followed her out and walked to our house.

Yolanda set up her books on the kitchen table, sat down and sighed. I took the note out of my pocket, unfolded it and held it in front of her face. "I found it," I said.

"What's the first number?" Lydia said from the living room, phone to her ear, one finger pointed at the dial. I called it out to her and went to the living room. Yolanda followed. I knew she would.

"No answer. Next?"

Lydia found out Philipa would be at work at seven that night.

"I don't know why you don't like me," Yolanda said.

"It's not about like. It's about your mother dumping you. Doesn't it bother you?" I said.

"If she doesn't want me, why should I go back?" Yolanda said.

"Shirleen doesn't want me either but here I am until I finish high school."

"If she didn't want you," Lydia said, "she should've kept her legs closed." Yolanda stomped to the kitchen with a pout while Lydia and I giggled.

Lydia lifted her books from the console TV then stared at the pictures. She smiled and picked up my first grade picture. "You were so cute," she said. She set it down carefully in front of the picture of Shirleen and Joe Henry, turning it a little so it faced straight ahead. "I can't believe I never saw you . . . Are these your cousins or something?" She held out the Polaroid in the brass-colored frame.

"That's Shirleen and her brothers and sisters," I said. I had to remember to move my first grade picture to the back; the one of Shirleen and Joe Henry always sat in front.

"Oh," Lydia said. "I thought it was you because . . . Then who's the white-looking lady in the back? She's not related to you, is she?"

I shrugged. "Shirleen just puts it back when I pick it up."

Lydia looked at the Polaroid once more then spread her books across the floor. I left the Polaroid in the front but slid my first grade picture back so it was even with and not in front of Shirleen and Joe Henry.

"Your floors are so clean," Lydia said. "Your mom cleans every day?"

"Shirleen doesn't clean anything but herself," I said. Lydia laughed. "Yolanda and I clean all weekend, every morning after breakfast and all holidays, even Christmas and Thanksgiving though Yolanda was here this time so for once I wasn't in the kitchen all by myself while everybody else was watching TV and eating sweet potato pie and playing double dutch." I slammed my social studies book closed because my chest was too tight to breathe right.

"Ain't no way I'd clean up for her," Lydia said, talking about her own mother, I guessed. Lydia's shivery-looking mother was the same height as Lydia but narrower, not someone who could take a Sock It to Me to Lydia for fifteen minutes to make her stand at a sink cutting okra. "That's her damn job, not mine."

"So what is your job?" I said.

Lydia stopped and looked up from her books. "To go to school." She said she cleaned her room only because she liked it that way and no one, not even her mother, was allowed in. I stared at her, wondering where the Pig made her do what he did—in their bedroom, the boys' room, on the sofa in the pile of clothes.

Shirleen came home. She shifted the grocery bag from one

arm to another. "So, another orphan?" she said with a smile.

Lydia looked at her with a serious face. "I'm doing my homework."

"Well, it's almost dark, dear, how will you get home?" Shirleen tried to sound nice but I could tell she didn't like Lydia or at least didn't like Lydia in the house. In the whole time I'd gone to St. John's, I had never brought a friend home, never been allowed to bring a friend home. I felt scared, ready to defend myself after Lydia left because I knew Shirleen would have a lot to say, or a little to say with Sock It to Me as punctuation.

"I'll walk," Lydia said. She tried to sound nice, too, but I could hear and feel she didn't mean it. I hoped she was looking at Shirleen and seeing the woman who beat me because a pervert shoved my hand in his pants.

"That's too dangerous."

"Just as dangerous as daytime," I said.

"Sandi, please . . ."

"Sandi? Who's Sandi?" Lydia said. Shirleen cocked her head and gave Lydia a tight-lipped smile. "Who's name is that?"

"It's a nickname," Shirleen said stiffly.

"It's stupid. Besides she doesn't like it because that fat you-know-what called her that to be mean so I don't see why you use it." Before Lydia finished, Shirleen walked back to the kitchen. Lydia and I smiled wide and tried not to laugh.

Lydia stacked her books. She put her keys in her fist, like she had shown me. I let her out.

I tapped Shirleen on the shoulder and showed her the note with Philipa's number on it. She took it with a surprised face. "Where'd you get this?" she said.

"From Dad."

"Oh."

"Actually, he gave it to Yolanda and she hid it."

"I can understand why."

"She'll be at work at seven," I said.

By seven, I was in the tub, writing in my diary. I hadn't written in it since Lydia's note.

When I came out, the towel wrapped around me, feeling almost too clean, I saw Shirleen and Yolanda on the sofa, Yolanda in Shirleen's lap, and I thought I heard crying. Shirleen patted the sofa next to her and I sat even though the towel around me was damp and I'd catch hell if the sofa got mildewed. "We called," Shirleen said.

"And?"

Shirleen raised her eyebrows. "Whatever she told Yolanda made her . . . " And she nodded her head at Yolanda curled on her lap. I should've been jealous, Shirleen was my mother, but I wasn't. She could have Shirleen. She needed her more. "And what she said to me? What a mouth." Shirleen covered Yolanda's ear and lowered her voice. "She said she would pay me anything to keep her. She's 'too busy,' she said. How can you be too busy for your own child?"

"How can you."

"It was your big idea to call," Shirleen said. Yolanda cried harder and Shirleen cuddled her closer. "Are you happy now that she's miserable?" she said, nodding at Yolanda shaking in her lap.

I put on my pajamas. It was warm and sticky and smelled like rain. I remembered Mamalita standing in her front yard watching the sky, telling me it would rain soon and me running for the clothesline. We raced to get the clothes down, dropping clothespins in the grass and laughing, shaking out clothes that fell, and standing together at the screen door to watch the rain. I dreamed of sitting on the porch during the heavy storm, snapping beans with Mamalita. The water splashed everywhere except on us. We didn't talk. I just felt her presence behind me in the rocking chair. When I looked down at myself, the rosary I'd made hung around my neck. And Mamalita whispered that I could find it if I looked hard enough.

• • •

Every class made red, white and blue banners, paintings of flags, and all kinds of red, white and blue papier maché things for the Bicentennial; the eighth grade girls would do a play, the girls playing all the Founding Fathers, and Lydia had been busy practicing after school three days a week. In second grade, Yolanda and all the girls traced and cut out paper dolls of Betsy Ross, Martha Washington, Abigail Adams and Molly Pitcher with red, white and blue clothes. Sixth grade had designed a paper flag to hang in the hall, a map of the United States colored like the flag. Miss Boudreaux had the girls paint one side, the boys the other. The girls peeked at the boys and asked for more paint when we already had some just to be able to talk to them or watch them walk to the supply closet. I couldn't see anything in a boy's walk that was interesting. When I thought of boys I thought of cocks and when I thought of cocks I thought of billy clubs. I still hadn't read the rest of Lydia's note. She said the rest was about the insides I needed to protect.

• • •

Lydia was pale and shaky at recess. "Sister Michael!" I said. Sister had the collar of a boy in each hand and whirled them around when she turned to look at me. I pointed to Lydia. "She's sick!"

"Take her to the office!" Sister said. I took Lydia's arm and we went up the stairs to Sister Paul's office. Sister Mary Clare wasn't in the front office nor was the secretary. I knocked on Sister Paul's door and we went in.

Sister Paul sat behind her desk. The top was very neat, just a black phone, typewriter, a paperback New Testament like we read in religion class, a ledger, one pencil and red, blue and black pens. Sister Paul was smaller than Sister Mary Clare and the skin of her face looked rough and old though her green eyes were bright and round. She waited. "Yes, girls."

Lydia started crying. Sister Paul's face didn't change; she waited longer while Lydia rubbed her face with tissues. "Okay, okay," she said. "My stepfather." She looked at Sister Paul and Sister's expression changed just a little, like she could tell she'd hear something bad. Lydia said, "He makes me, he puts his . . . privates into my mouth and makes me swallow and he said he was gonna make me do more because I'm getting older and bigger and he looks at me and he made me . . ." Lydia dropped her head.

Sister jumped up from her chair and closed the door. She sat in a chair next to Lydia, so Lydia was between us and asked a lot of questions, using words I never thought I'd hear a nun say, like "penis," "vagina," "anal" and "ejaculate," a word for the sour stuff that came out of penises.

Sister suddenly looked at me like she'd forgotten I was there. "Sandrine, go to class."

"No, please, let her stay," Lydia said. Sister Paul gently touched Lydia's shoulder then went out to the front office.

At lunchtime, Sister Paul brought up three trays, one for each of us. She asked Lydia more questions. Then we ate in silence. She didn't say anything when I didn't drink my milk. I took our trays downstairs and by the time I got back, Lydia's mother and stepfather were sitting by the secretary's desk, waiting. The secretary stole glances at them like they were straight from hell and would take her if she studied them too long. Sister Mary Clare sat at her desk by Sister Paul's door, slowly typing a letter, her back stiffer than usual.

As soon as I closed Sister Paul's door, Lydia grabbed my hand and pulled me down into the chair next to hers. Her hands were icy cold and I could feel her shaking. "They're outside?" she said. I nodded. She moaned and her eyes got wet. Sister Paul came close and pressed Lydia's head against her hip.

"Shh," Sister Paul said.

Then Lydia's parents came in. The Pig was my father's color but in the bright sun and fluorescent light of Sister Paul's office, I could tell he was white. Lydia's mother looked as pale and sick and worried as Lydia; the circles around her eyes made her look hollow, like her voice would echo out of a deep cave

"Did something happen?" Lydia's mother said before she sat down in the chair closest to Sister Paul's desk.

"Yes, something has happened but not here at school," Sister Paul said, looking at the Pig.

The Pig slumped in his chair. "Sister, I gotta get back to work some time."

"Okay," said Sister, still looking at him. "The quick version, Mrs. Petitjean, is your husband has been molesting your daughter and you must do something about it."

"What?" Lydia's mother said. She glared at Lydia. "How dare you . . ."

"Lydia," Sister Paul said loudly, "has attended this school since kindergarten and I have never known her to lie. And she knows things no girl her age would know unless she has been violated by an adult male."

Lydia's mother whined and wailed. My stomach flipped. The Pig snorted. "She probably learned it from boys, little slut."

"Excuse me, Mr. Petitjean, none of my girls are 'sluts.' Besides, sluts are made by man, not born of woman."

Lydia's mother jumped out of her chair and started punching Lydia in the face, screaming, "Filthy liar!" over and over. I hid Lydia's head with my body, her mother's bony, hard punches on my back and neck until Sister Paul pushed Mrs. Petitjean back into a chair. Sister Paul grabbed the Pig's arm and pushed him into a chair, too. I couldn't believe the little nun was so strong.

"Girls," Sister Paul said, "go wait with Sister Mary Clare."

As soon as we stepped out, Sister Mary Clare led us down the hall to an empty classroom. The secretary fetched ice from the cafeteria and Sister Mary Clare held it against Lydia's red swollen cheek while Lydia cried. I was breathing hard and fast, feeling lightheaded. We heard heavy footsteps in the hall. Lydia looked up and I got up to go to the door. Sister Mary Clare blocked my path. "Sit down, Sandrine." I did. "You girls have seen too much already," she said in a very quiet voice, her eyes filling with tears. Lydia and I looked at each other, shocked that Sister Mary Clare, the one who punished boys, whose voice carried during assemblies to shut everyone up, who watched the lunch lines like a falcon, seemed so soft. I threw my arms around her waist. She held me to one side, Lydia to the other, while footsteps shuffled and scraped on the wood floor in the hall.

Sister Mary Clare sat us in desks next to her and let us lay our heads on her shoulders while she read to us the stories of Saint Michael, the saint Lydia got her confirmation name from, St. Catherine de Ricci, who had mystical spells every week for twelve years, then mini stories of female saints whose names I might consider for my own confirmation—Agatha, Agnes, Angela, Bernadette, Cecilia, Maria Goretti, Margaret, Martha, and Sister's favorite, Clare, who founded the Poor Clares and who St. Augustine said could live as they pleased, without possessions, without alms, just purity, ruled by themselves and not men. Sister told me I would wear a white dress that came down almost to my ankles, a special hairdo and brand new white shoes to a special confirmation Mass.

The door opened and all three of us stood. It was Shirleen and Sister Paul. I ran to Shirleen and hugged her. "Okay, let's go home," Shirleen said quietly.

"Can Lydia come?"

Sister Paul patted my shoulder. "Lydia will stay with us tonight," she said.

"Where?" I said.

Sister Paul smiled. "Sisters live in houses, too, you know." Shirleen smiled at Sister Paul and led me out. I looked back at Lydia and waved. She looked sad but not as scared. I wondered where her mother was, if she'd gone to jail with the Pig. In the car I told Shirleen how Lydia's mother had hit her in the face, called her a liar.

"Some women are like that," Shirleen said as we turned onto our block. "They choose their husbands over their children."

"But where will Lydia go? Will she just stay with the nuns?"

"No, Sandi, we do not have room for one more."

• • •

Lydia went home the next week. She said her mother stopped going to work, just stayed on the sofa all day with the TV on and wouldn't look at her. Lydia's brothers, without their mother to yell at them or the Pig to slap them, tore through the house all day; most days Lydia couldn't get them dressed in time for school and left them home. She said it was better with the nuns. In the two-story brick house next to the school, it was perfectly quiet, she had a narrow little room to herself and slept like a rock, they had toast and coffee for breakfast and soup and bread for dinner, and each nun in the house gave her something when she left—a rosary, a prayer book, a bible, medals, scapulars. Lydia had two scapulars around her neck and two other medals pinned to the insides of her clothes. She said she had never been treated so kindly in her whole life.

· · ·

Two cars of men most afternoons slowed down to say something, even if it was just Hey or Lookin' good or Lemme holla atcha. I said we would make them stop the next time they yelled. Lydia liked the idea.

At a corner near Lydia's house where the sidewalk was cracked and crumbling, Lydia and I got chunks of concrete and hid them in our purses. Then we saw one of the cars, a dull gold Pontiac with three men inside. They slowed down and we saw them looking at us.

"Yolanda, shake your butt at them," Lydia said. Yolanda put a big grin on her face and turned to wiggle at them. Lydia and I waved and smiled. The tires squealed as the car turned the corner and soon we heard the motor revving around the block and back to us. We smiled and waved.

"Hey, there," the man on the passenger side said. "Hey, hey, hey, y'all wanna ride with us?"

"Yeah, I got some candy for you, girl!" the man in the back seat said, leaning out the back window.

"What kind of candy?" Yolanda said.

"Only the best," he said, showing a gold tooth.

"Fuck off!" Lydia yelled and we started throwing pieces of concrete at the car. They all ducked as we threw until we cracked the rear windshield into webs and the car took off fast. "Sons of bitches!" I said.

Then we ran home before they or anyone else could stop us.

· · ·

My skirts were shorter. When I looked at myself in the bathroom mirror at recess, I was as tall as some of the girls in my class. I wore my hair in two buns mostly, twists or braids wrapped and pinned behind each ear, and it made me look older than ten. I guessed that's what men looked at. Though Champ knew exactly how old I was and my stomach griped as I thought that some of the men following us also knew exactly how old we were. Lydia's note was getting worn and soft from shifting around in my purse. She told me it wasn't so important to read the last page now as later, before I turned twelve.

When Lydia came to do her homework, I made her something to eat, too, a sandwich, a can of soup like chicken and stars that Shirleen didn't like and wouldn't miss, or leftovers, because with the Pig gone and her mother still on the sofa, there was hardly any food in the house and any food she was able to make, the boys devoured. Lydia worried about them as much as she called them names; at least they got lunch at school, when they went to school, she said. They had plucked all the roses off the bushes around the Virgin Mary statue, dug holes in the yard, and cracked their bedroom door slamming it repeatedly. Her mother didn't even complain about the door slamming. Lydia's face was hard and angry when she talked about her mother. I knew how she felt.

• • •

Shirleen said she wouldn't take us to any night parades because she was too tired after work, we couldn't go to parades Saturday morning or afternoon because that was the only day we cleaned our house and Mother Dear's house since the weekdays were filled with homework, wouldn't take us to ones on Saturday night because if we stayed up too late we'd miss church Sunday morning, and all Sunday parades were out of the question because it was her only day to rest. Then she sipped her coffee and looked at the newspaper, like she'd told us to put our plates in the sink, not erased the entire Carnival season. She noticed me looking at her and pursed her lips. "What now, Sandi?"

"It must be nice to be an adult," I said. Shirleen smiled a little. "You don't have to care about other people, especially children." Her smile stiffened. "I guess we have to wait our turn to have people smaller than us to be cruel to. But I could be cruel to you, Yolanda, since you're smaller and you could probably push around some kindergartners—"

"Shut up," Shirleen said.

"No, I will not," I said. "You just sat there and told us we'll see no parades this year because you don't feel like being bothered and cleaning Mother Dear's clean house is more important than these two weeks, just two weeks out of the year, two weeks, two weeks!" Her mouth was pinched and dry and her eyes started to narrow. "You can't pretend I matter for two weeks?"

She swung at me and missed. I put my bowl in the sink, got my books and left. I walked slowly and Yolanda was able to catch up before I reached Lydia's house.

"Why you make her so mad?" Yolanda said.

"She made me mad," I said. "She started it. She always does."

"She's nice to me."

"Because you're not hers and she figures you'll leave one day. Me, she can't stand 'cause I'm hers for life."

"You can have my mama," Yolanda said, her head down.

"I don't want yours. She's worse than Shirleen. You have every right to hate her. I hate her for you. I hate her for Dad, too."

Lydia waited for us on the porch. The grass was long and weeds grew almost as tall as the waist of the Mary statue. Lydia's brothers busted out the door, left it open and climbed over the fence to run to school. I was glad none of them were in sixth grade. Lydia shook her head and locked the front door.

"If that woman doesn't get her sorry ass off that . . . " Lydia said. We walked a block. "Even if she got up it wouldn't make a difference," Lydia said. "She yells, they yell back, and that was when the Pig would slap them and they'd act right for a little while. I wish the girls' schools were still cloistered."

"Cloistered?" Yolanda said.

"Like nuns. They used to lock the gates and doors and only let you go home for holidays. I'd love that," Lydia said.

• • •

Lydia went to Sister Paul's office every Monday during lunch. She said she told Sister Paul everything, about the Pig, about her mother, about the boys and going to my house to do homework and her worry that she wouldn't get a scholarship to Dominican and get out of the house. She said Sister Paul mostly listened then they would pray to Saint Maria Goretti or Saint Joan of Arc or pray the whole rosary, even if Lydia was late for class. I was thinking about Lydia and Sister Paul praying the rosary when we passed Mother Dear's yard and I remembered Mamalita telling me in my dream that I could find the rosary I made if I looked for it.

"Sandi?" Yolanda said. I was staring into Mother Dear's yard. I looked up at her and Lydia on our porch, watching me. "You coming?" Yolanda said, her eyes big and almost scared.

I gave her my books and purse. "I need to look for something."

I took a lot of deep breaths to calm my stomach; it felt like I would vomit all over the wall and fence and sidewalk. But I thought Mamalita meant the rosary or some of the beads were there somewhere. I couldn't remember it breaking. I didn't remember it at all until a week after. In the dirt under the fence, I saw something shine, like a bit of glass. One pearly white bead stuck in the dirt. I dug it out with my fingernail, blew dirt out of the hole in the center and slipped it in my purse. I couldn't look anymore. When I got inside I took a bath before homework. I needed to feel clean.

· · ·

We finished our English lesson early so Miss Boudreaux let us start our homework. We had twenty-five minutes to the bell and since I stayed in the room to do homework while I waited for Lydia, I had almost an hour. Miss Boudreaux let some of them sit in pairs and a couple of girls asked me for help with math problems. Then David Casimir pushed a desk next to mine, blocking me in when he sat down. He had his math book. "Hey, can you help me with this?"

He opened his math book. I took a deep breath and said, "No, absolutely not."

"Why not? You're really good at—"

"I will not help you." I noticed a pair of chocolate girls peeking back at us and grinning. "Get away from me. Don't talk to me anymore."

"What I do?"

I looked at him and couldn't believe he was still there. "You are causing problems for me, I will not help you now or ever so just go the hell away from me." He didn't move fast enough so I slammed my hand on his desk. "Go!"

"Sandrine Miller!" Miss Boudreaux stood up behind her desk.

"Get away from me," I said to David.

"Office, Sandrine."

I picked up all my books and stomped off to the office ahead of Miss Boudreaux. She went into Sister Paul's office then came out and sent me in.

"We meet again," Sister Paul said without a smile.

I folded my arms and didn't answer. Sister Paul sat back in her chair and waited. The final bell rang and we still waited. The clock was behind me but I thought if I moved she could make me talk. The hall filled with voices and footsteps then finally was quiet.

"Sandrine," Sister Paul said. "What's wrong with helping David with one math problem?"

"I'm not on top of the honor roll." Sister Paul leaned back and looked down at her desk. She never looked away, even when Lydia had told her about the Pig's penis choking her and him holding her ears. I felt mad. I felt she knew. "I get better grades. I've gotten one C the whole time I been here but he's on the Alpha roll for sixth grade and I'm on the Beta. I need a scholarship more than he does. He's a boy, he'll always be a boy, this is my only chance." Then I cried so hard I forgot Sister Paul was there, couldn't catch my breath, felt my head pounding. My stomach turned inside out. I jumped when Sister Paul touched my shoulder and offered me a handful of tissues I could barely see through my tears. I used almost half the box before I could breathe and see and when I looked at Sister Paul's face, her eyes green like stained glass and kind like Sister Lawrence's, I felt sorry for being so rude and tears came back to my eyes.

"Sandrine," she said. "What's upsetting you?"

"Everything," I said.

She put the box of tissues on her lap. "You've had an upsetting year. Do you pray? At night?"

I hung my head. "No."

"Why not?"

"Because if God cared," I said, "He would've helped me. But

He didn't. So He's either not there or He loves only little children who don't ask questions or talk back."

She wrapped her arms around me, pulling me and the chair closer. I wanted to struggle, to get away from her, to go home with Lydia and Yolanda, do my homework, but then I relaxed against Sister Paul. Her habit smelled freshly washed and she spoke so quietly and gently I felt I had to listen. "God loves us all the time. God isn't like Superman, He can't fly in and beat up the bad guys but He is there when you need him most, afterwards, to heal you and your heart." She sat me up and looked at me. She smiled. "God knows you are strong. And God will punish Lydia's stepfather. Believe that, Sandrine. God does love us. It can be hard to feel His love through our own pain and suffering but He is there. Always. It's like with parents. We think at times our parents don't love us but they always do. Sometimes it's hard to see."

She gave me a prayer book with a Saint Clare bookmark and a Joan of Arc plastic medal on red ribbon, like one of the scapulars Lydia wore around her neck and said she never took off, even for baths. I left wondering where the nuns got all their scapulars, prayer books, bookmarks and Bibles. By the time I got outside, Yolanda and Lydia were gone. I walked home alone, slowly, down Broad Street, looking through the prayer book. There were prayers for getting a good night's sleep, for arthritis, for terminal illness, for the morning and afternoon and evening, and different prayers to say over the rosary but no prayers for skin stinging from Sock It to Me or against hairy penises.

I sat on the sofa. Yolanda came from the kitchen. "Lydia went home," she said.

"Do you believe in God?"

"Yeah."

"Why?"

"Because He made the earth and sky."

"That's all?"

Yolanda's eyes looked back and forth while she thought then she smiled. "Yeah."

"Don't forget your homework."

"Okay." She went back to the kitchen. I was still on the sofa when Shirleen came home. Shirleen didn't say anything. She felt the TV as she walked past.

"No, I was not watching TV," I said.

"I didn't say anything," Shirleen said.

"You didn't have to." I jumped to my feet. "I don't know what it is with you," I heard myself say.

"Lord, here we go again," Shirleen said.

"You treat me like I am evil, not like evil followed me. And I remember the look on your face, like you always knew I'd turn out bad."

"Sandi ..."

I barricaded the bedroom door. I had a lot of money buried under the house. I looked through my drawers and found the letter with Dad's address and phone number, under a jar of jelly. He was living out in the country, near a clinic, driving Philipa's car. I imagined lots of trees, small wood houses, gardens, cows and chickens, homemade ice cream in summer and vegetables to can in the fall.

• • •

I started a letter to Dad. After I wrote "Dear Dad," I stopped, unsure where to start, so I folded the paper and kept it in my purse. During science, I wrote about Shirleen whipping me for doing my homework. While we waited for Lydia, I added a page from my notebook to write about Shirleen not taking us to any parades this year.

Yolanda sat near me. "What you writing?" she said.

I folded the paper and tucked it in my purse.

I didn't tell Lydia about it, the money and the letter the only things I hadn't told her since we became friends. When Shirleen came home, I went into the bedroom and pushed the dresser against the door. Shirleen tried to come in and when it didn't open, it sounded like she kicked it.

"Goddammit, Sandi," she said. "Open the fucking door."

"I need some privacy, I'll—"

"You are not old enough to need privacy. Open the door."

"How old do you have to be to need privacy?" I said then I thought to write it in the letter. While Shirleen was knocking and kicking on the door, I was smiling and writing that question then writing Dad about Shirleen never believing Champ followed Yolanda and me, still didn't believe he had ever followed us. I felt sick. I got the rosary Sister Lawrence gave me and held it in my left hand tight enough to numb it. I told him about Champ pulling down my panties and leaving zipper scratches on my wrist; they had healed, leaving light brown spots behind. I told him about not being on the honor roll because a boy from my class was on top though my grades were better. I told him about Lydia and her mother punching us. I tried to think of and write down everything unfair, frightening, mean and cruel that had happened since the summer. He thought Mister Tom was bad.

I rewrote the letter several times that week. I took out a lot of the stuff about Shirleen but I wrote more about her beating me and calling me a slut. The only things I wrote about school were Lydia's parents and the honor roll. And I told him that when he came to see me, I realized how nice he really was and how much I liked and loved him.

• • •

We missed all the parades the first week of Carnival, even Saturday and Sunday. I asked Shirleen why we had to miss the Sunday parades after doing homework Friday and Mother Dear's house and laundry Saturday. Her answer was a post-church list of chores. While we mopped and dusted and washed and dried and put away, she went out, not telling us where.

That night, Endymion would pass a few blocks from the house, late at night, right after bedtime and I wanted to sneak out to it but it was just the kind of place I'd see Champ or some other man who'd seen Yolanda, Lydia and me walking along Broad St. and if something happened, I could never tell Shirleen.

The day had been warmer than usual and the house was still thick and humid that night. When I pulled on my pajamas they stuck to my skin. I didn't fall asleep, thinking about parades and which deep voice would return with Shirleen that night.

I must've fallen asleep because I heard Shirleen's voice without hearing her come in. By her voice—angry, defensive—I could tell she was talking to my dad. I tiptoed to the bedroom doorway to hear her better.

"No, I did not . . . You . . . " She was quiet. "What's to understand? Are you calling me a liar? You don't know anything about . . . " She was quiet a long time. I heard a creak and groan, like she'd flopped onto the sofa. "No," she said loudly, "not at all." Then a muffled chime and plastic slamming into plastic. I heard her footsteps and had just covered myself with the sheet when the door flung open.

"Sandrine," she said. "Get up and come here."

"I got school tomorrow," I said.

"Do what I say and come here!"

Her voice was shaky, like she wasn't just mad at me but scared, too. I felt as shaky as her voice; Dad must've gotten my letter. Yolanda woke up suddenly and watched me with big eyes.

I followed Shirleen to the dark living room.

"Your father," she said, pointing toward the phone. "He says you sent him a letter that proves I am incapable of caring for you. You told him I don't give you an allowance anymore?"

"I told him you gave it to Yolanda for getting Cs—"

She slapped me. "Stupid, selfish bitch! I gave it to Yolanda to encourage her. Like an allowance is more than feeding you, putting clothes on your back, sending you to Catholic school, putting up with your shit—How dare you tell him I 'beat' you." She raised her hand again. I flinched, hated myself for it and stood up straight, eyes half-closed and waiting for the next blow. "You don't know what a beating is," she said, her voice low and growling.

She turned her back on me since she didn't have a door to slam in my face. I got a cold towel for my cheek and got back into bed. I didn't feel like crying or yelling. I just held the towel to my cheek until the stinging stopped then I went to sleep.

In the morning my cheek was reddish purple. When I smiled, the skin prickled, like it had been burned. Yolanda said I should cover it with baby powder. I wanted to make it redder with Shirleen's makeup but I never went near her things in the living room anymore; when we had to clean, I made Yolanda do the living room so I wouldn't spit in Shirleen's Nadinola or dip her lipstick in the toilet.

• • •

Friday morning we woke to a car blowing its horn. I rolled over and pulled the covers tighter around my neck. I heard Shirleen's heavy footsteps come to the door of our room. "Wake up, it's your father," she said. I opened my eyes. I nudged Yolanda.

"Did she say it's Dad?" I said.

"That's what I heard," Yolanda said with a big grin.

We ran to the living room, looked out the window and saw

Philipa's big green car parked in Mother Dear's driveway and Dad walking up our steps with a grocery bag. He had a big smile on his face. His afro was cut close to his head and with the smile, his white shirt and khaki pants, he looked like a boy from school.

"Watch, he's gonna take us to some parades," I said.

Yolanda and I let Dad in and hugged him and asked how long he could stay. He gave me an extra hug and whispered he was glad to see me. I felt warm and happy and safe. We helped him make breakfast—pancakes, bacon, eggs. If he'd made toast I would've brought out one of my jelly jars. It smelled so good Shirleen came out of the bathroom where she'd spent an extra long time getting ready, avoiding us more than primping since she looked like she always did. Dad said good morning to her, she said so back, not looking at him.

"So," Dad said. "What happened to your friend's father?"

Shirleen rolled her eyes and sighed impatiently. I turned to Dad. "I think he went to jail," I said. "He's not in—"

"Okay, enough about that," Shirleen said. "It's over and done, just forget it."

"How can she just forget it when she sees the girl every day?" Dad said. "How can she just—"

"Shh." Shirleen said, hissing like a pierced balloon. "She's nine years old, just drop it."

"Ten," Yolanda and I said at the same time.

"How is she supposed to cope," Dad said, his face turning red, "if you insist on—"

"Cope?" Shirleen said. "Cope? Who's got time for that namby-pamby privileged shit? Down here in the real world, Dr. Miller, you get up in the morning and put your panties on whether they dirty or not. You don't know half the shit she's done," she added, looking hard at me.

"Jesus Christ," Dad said. He turned his chair so he couldn't see her face. I felt nervous but I also felt like cheering Dad on. "You won't be late for school, will you?" he said to me.

"A little."

"I'll give you a ride."

"Really?" We only got rides from Shirleen when it was raining hard and she dropped us off on her way to work, half an hour before school started. Yolanda and I ran to get ready.

When he pulled up to the school, Lydia was standing by the entrance, talking to an eighth-grade girl. Yolanda got out first. Dad touched my arm.

"I got your letter."

"Shirleen told me. She's furious."

"She's embarrassed," Dad said. "This summer, no stepmother, no chores, and you can stay if you want."

"Stay?"

"There's a good school, bookmobile, a great doctor." He smiled and I smiled, too. Then he shook his head and spoke quietly, to himself or me or both, I wasn't sure. "I want you to have some childhood before it's too late. You better get to school."

The bell had rung and only Lydia was outside, staring into the car. "My dad," I said to Lydia. She nodded but still looked suspicious. "He's really okay. I might go live with him," I said. At recess I wanted to ask Lydia what she thought but it didn't seem right to ask her. She probably would've said not to; she warned me more and more often about Mister Albert, the seventh-grade teacher, to watch how he looked at me and called on me in class but I didn't think he was at all suspicious. He was a teacher, not some guy in a car or the Pig, but Lydia didn't see that. She said she hoped there were no male teachers at Dominican, not even priests or deacons.

I also couldn't ask Yolanda what she thought. I didn't

want her to come but I didn't want her to stay with Shirleen. I felt Shirleen should be alone, that she'd be happier that way, except for the housework. I imagined never writing or calling her and her never writing or calling me. It made me feel sad. But I was still angry at her. And she still didn't think much of me. Straight As, housework, walking myself to school since I was five, taking care of myself and Yolanda didn't add up for Shirleen like I felt it should. My stomach was upset all day and I managed to give away my lunch without Sister Mary Clare seeing. I told myself it would be good for Yolanda, good for Shirleen, good for Dad. I felt guilty and happily excited and lonely and saved.

Dad was there to pick us up after school. Lydia didn't want a ride. I was ready to beg her to come when she started walking away. Dad had parked across the street in the church lot and walked over to me as Lydia started walking away.

"Is that your friend?" Dad said.

"Yeah," I said. "She didn't want a ride. She thinks . . ."

Champ's red car turned the corner and honked at Lydia who didn't stop, speed up or seem to notice. It felt like my empty stomach turned upside down as Champ's car got closer and I could see he was staring directly at me. "Hey, yella," he said with a wink. He puckered up his lips at me, stopped the car and leaned out the window. I was frozen. "What, no kiss for your sugar daddy today?"

Dad stepped closer to me and I jumped, at first forgetting it was him and that he was even there. "You don't look like her daddy to me," Dad said.

Champ's forehead wrinkled up and he squinted at my dad. "And who the hell are you?"

Dad stepped toward the car and Champ peeled away from the curb. I didn't know if he realized the man with me was my dad or if the sick jerk thought Dad was my new sugar daddy who I let shove my hand in his pants.

When we got in Dad's car, I realized it was the first time I'd been picked up from school; if it rained after school, we either waited for it to slow down or walked home and got wet because Shirleen didn't finish work until five. I felt only half-happy.

"Your friend Lydia thinks . . . ?"

"She thinks everybody is like the Pig."

"The Pig?" He snickered. "You come up with some names."

Shirleen's car was in Mother Dear's driveway so Dad could park in front of the house. She was inside, on the sofa when we came in, early; most of City Hall left early on parade days. She and Dad nodded at each other.

"Get your jeans, girls, 'cause we're going to the parades!" Dad said.

Yolanda jumped up and down. I saw Shirleen's face—eyes narrowed, mouth pinched tight. "What is it?" I said to her. She didn't move. "You think we don't deserve it?"

"All that traffic and yelling and garbage . . . not me," she said.

"Good," I said.

"Sandrine," Dad said.

I hung my head. I stepped closer to Shirleen and said, "Sorry." Shirleen didn't even look up. It seemed like she wanted to be anywhere else on earth.

"Get your homework done so we can get to the parades," Dad said.

"Okay!" Yolanda and I said.

Dad sat on the porch to read the paper, Yolanda took the kitchen table and I set my books on the living room floor, exactly between Shirleen on the sofa and her bed which smelled like bedsheets just taken off the clothesline. Shirleen stayed on the sofa, staring at the blank TV.

"I'm sorry," I said.

"For which?" Shirleen said.

I opened my books. "I'm sorry I made you feel this way," I said. "I had to stick up for myself."

She shook her head a little then shrugged. "Do you think you'll be happy with him?" I was surprised, I didn't think he'd told her and I wondered if Yolanda knew. "He works all the time. He doesn't know what it takes to raise a girl. All the watching and worrying and rules and going out looking for them ..."

"What are you talking about? You've never had to watch me or go looking for me like I'm 'running the streets,' as you say. I don't even know what that means. Watch what? Worry what? Who are you talking about?"

"He'll never tell you what you need to know about boys."

"I know what I need to know about boys," I said and bent my head over my homework.

"How could you know?"

"How can I not?"

● ● ●

Dad kept us out late at parades then woke us early to get ready for Saturday's. We packed sandwiches and sodas and bags of chips and stayed out all day, seeing parade after parade, and did the same on Sunday. We filled three grocery bags in Dad's trunk with beads and doubloons. Monday night Shirleen came with us. I think she wanted to supervise, like Dad was another child who couldn't keep us safe and she stood at the back of the crowd, grocery bags at her feet we filled with beads. We got up early Tuesday, had toast and pomegranate jelly for breakfast, radio playing Mardi Gras songs loud and even Shirleen sang "Iko Iko" with me and Yolanda while we made sandwiches for the day and packed the cooler. Every time I looked at Dad, he was smiling.

He said he hadn't had this many days off since he started working as a doctor. Shirleen hmphed.

With Dad on one end and Yolanda and I on the other, we carried the cooler to a place on Canal Street in front of Goudchaux's, the same spot where Dad had spent his first Mardi Gras, with Shirleen, Mother Dear and Uncle Jerry. Dad sat on the cooler between parades. My face hurt from grinning all day and by the last parade, I was hoarse from yelling. In the car, Yolanda had me pour one of the bags of beads and doubloons on her. She laughed and laughed.

Wednesday after church Dad took most of the beads with him. "They'll be waiting for you," he said. And he left with ashes on his forehead and beads in his cooler.

• • •

Lydia talked less and less. I guessed she was worried, waiting to hear from Dominican. She still saw Sister Paul once a week but she didn't talk about it anymore. Her mother was off the sofa but not working and she suspected her mother had had contact with the Pig, a letter or call or even visit. Lydia didn't know where he was. After her parents came to Sister Paul's office, Lydia talked to a policeman then a family court judge who told her the best thing was to keep him away from the house but there was nothing he or anyone else could do to put the Pig in jail, that they needed more than her word against his. I think all she prayed for was admission and a full scholarship.

I read the rest of Lydia's note, the last page, the outer layer of the packet, peppered with thinned-out spots and a few holes. There was a lot inside to protect. But now I knew what I needed to know about boys, about myself, what Champ wanted to do to me, and Shirleen hadn't told me any of it.

• • •

The sixth, seventh and eighth grade girls did the Stations of the Cross together on Fridays, after lunch instead of recess, smelling like fish sticks. Instead of saying the prayers, I stared at the stained glass windows, glowing in the dim church. Between them were Stations carved into the walls but they were dull, the colors faded and flaking off, much just gray stone. The folds of clothes carved in the stone were nice but I preferred the windows. I thought about what confirmation name I might choose next year—Joan of Arc, dressed as a man and an equal in battle and, near the end, after a day and night in a dress in jail, refused to wear it again even though it got her closer to the stake; St. Monica who wiped Christ's sweaty, bloody face and was rewarded with his image on her piece of cloth; St. Lawrence who, burning over a pit, joked that he was done on that side and needed flipping; St. Clare; or St. Mary Magdalene who went from prostitute to Christ's favorite. Sister Mary Joseph, the eighth-grade teacher, hurried me from Station to Station until I caught up with the rest.

Then Lydia missed two days of school. Her mother opened the door just enough to see us and say Lydia wasn't going, no other explanation before she closed the door and we heard it lock. At recess I was alone. The other sixth-grade girls, who hadn't talked to me much before, turned their faces away from me now that I was friends with an eighth-grader though I might have been able to get away with it if Lydia was black.

The third morning I sent Yolanda on to school alone and stayed to knock at Lydia's door. I had to see her. I'd started to worry. I'd even dreamed she had come with me to Mississippi instead of Yolanda.

Lydia's mother opened the door enough to show her nose, most of her mouth and one eye. "She's not going," she said.

"Is she sick? Can I see her? So I can get her homework?"

Lydia's mother didn't know I wasn't in the same class.

She blinked her eye slowly, like she'd fall asleep at the door. "Well. . . ." She opened the door wide enough for me to squeeze in.

It was dark and quiet. I guessed the boys were already at school. It smelled musty, like sweaty people had been closed up in the house a long time. Her mother turned up the TV and sat on the sofa. I knocked on Lydia's door.

"Go away!" Lydia sounded sick.

"Lydia?" I said.

The door opened. Lydia's face looked puffy and pale, like she was sick or had been crying a lot. She grabbed my wrist, pulled me in the room and slammed the door. Her room was neat and the curtains were open to let in lots of sunlight. The floor was clean and shiny. Her butterscotch walls glowed like sunshine in a picture but Lydia herself was sad and dark. She pulled me to the bed and we sat down. She pointed at a letter on her nightstand. "I heard," she said.

I held my breath, like it was my life, not hers, at stake.

"I got in." I cheered. "But I only got a partial scholarship and that woman says she will not pay for the rest because she has four boys to put through school." Lydia sobbed and cried hard for a few minutes. "She won't even call or go to the school to tell them, to try to. I'm gonna have to go to John Mac. John Mac! I got As to go to John Mac?"

"But . . ."

"I'll never get out of here, never. Whatever she has is going to the boys, she said. Because I broke her heart." Lydia blew her nose and was smiling when she threw the wad of tissue in the garbage can. "I broke her heart. *I* broke *her* heart." Lydia started pacing.

"Are you coming?"

"Maybe tomorrow."

I left her lying on her sunflower-dotted bedspread, staring out the window, sniffling and sighing. My chest felt heavy. At recess I looked through my prayer book for a prayer for her but couldn't find one. I didn't believe the prayers worked but the right one could help her feel better and at least get her to tell Sister Paul.

During religion, Father McNeeley sent me to the office to pick up mimeographs. Sister Mary Clare wasn't at her desk and the secretary was gone. Sister Paul's office door was half open and I heard typing. I got the stack of candy-sweet papers off the secretary's desk and knocked on Sister Paul's open door.

"Who's that out there?" she said without stopping her typing. She glanced at me as I opened the door more. "Oh, hold it a minute." She finished typing the page, pulled it out with a satisfied smile and turned her smile to me. "Sandrine. How have you been?"

I wanted to tell her about my dad's visit and moving away even if I had to pay for it myself. "Lydia."

"Yes?"

"She didn't get a big enough scholarship. She's at home, crying. She hasn't been sick. Her mother won't talk to anyone about it and says she won't pay for anything."

Sister Paul's brow furrowed. "Thank you, Sandrine." I didn't move. Sister Paul smiled gently. "Go back to class. I'll see what I can do."

I left then came back. "Thank you, Sister."

Sister Paul gave me a big smile and waved me off. I had more faith in Sister Paul than prayers.

• • •

Yolanda failed another spelling test so I promised to help her study for the end of the year. We didn't stop at Lydia's that day though I wanted to tell her I'd told Sister Paul and everything would be okay now because Sister Paul would make Lydia's mother call the school or make the Pig pay. I spent an hour helping Yolanda then did my own homework through dinner. Shirleen didn't talk to me much anymore. She seemed tired, or sad. Maybe Dad was right and she was embarrassed.

· · ·

I sent Yolanda on to school alone and knocked on Lydia's door. Her mother opened the door just enough to see me. "She's not here," she said.

"Did she go to school?"

"She left this." A folded piece of paper stuck out of the crack in the door. I took it and the door closed.

I opened and read it as I walked the block. Lydia said she knew exactly what to do—run away, like I did. She'd write when she could, if she could.

I looked up. Yolanda waited for me at Columbus and Broad, where we crossed to school. I put the note in my purse, not sure I'd read it right, not sure it was true, sure she meant Sister Paul had set everything right. I heard a long whistle as I walked closer to Yolanda and though the hair on my arms stood up, I didn't look or react, didn't even talk to Yolanda or take her hand when we crossed the street. I went through school trying to ignore the note and what I thought it said. I didn't touch it again until I got home and had finished helping Yolanda practice her spelling words. I got myself a glass of cold water, opened all my books and notebooks to the right pages then fished Lydia's note out of my purse.

I'd read right. She said she had a cousin in Georgia she would try to get to. She would try to write. And that was all. No goodbye or I'll miss you or thank you or don't worry or keep studying. She was just gone. For the first time I worried about going to Mississippi and not coming back. I'd thought I'd have Lydia to write to, that I'd still have a friend. Now I was friendless and sure I'd make none at a new school—straight As, from out of town, doctor father, no mother, pale like white bread with no crust.

When Shirleen came home, I wanted to tell her about Lydia but knew she wouldn't care. After dinner I went to my room and started to write in my diary but after I wrote "Lydia ran away, maybe to Georgia," I didn't want to write anything else and just went to bed early.

• • •

Yolanda walked ahead while I walked slowly past Lydia's house. Since she'd been gone the grass had finally been cut, the rosebushes trimmed, the Virgin Mary freshly painted white and sky blue. But as the anger crept up my legs, it was Shirleen I was angry at.

A car slowed down and a man leaned out. "Hey, cutie."

The car was white with a green vinyl top and I hadn't seen the man driving before but the one leaning out was Champ, his funny-colored eyes happy, his hand reaching out to me. I took one step back, put my hand on my hip and glared at him. "What did you say to me?" I said.

"I said, hey, cutie," Champ said, flicking his eyes up and down me. The driver laughed.

"If you talk to me anymore, I will have to kill you," I said.

"What?" Champ said. They laughed loud and I felt my skin burn. Champ's eyes weren't happy anymore but narrow, his smile looking pasted on. "I ain't never heard—"

"I'm gonna have to kill you."

"Girl . . ."

"I'm gonna have to kill you!"

Champ opened the car door. My chest got hot and quivery. My hands shook so I made fists.

"Aw, c'mon, man, leave her be," the driver said. He leaned over Champ to look at me. "She can't be but thirteen." The car started rolling. Champ closed the door and pointed at me as they drove away. I shook so much I barely made it home.

I dug up my money before dinner, when my stomach was empty. It hurt like I was being stabbed but I had nothing to throw up and dry heaves didn't stop me digging. Right before I opened the can to check the money, I felt a head-cracking fear that Dad would not be where he said he was, that when I showed up with Yolanda, he would look through me and close the door. I hid the can in my shirt and tiptoed into the house. I heard Shirleen talking to Yolanda while I was locked in the bathroom counting the money. I was still rich.

Catfish for dinner again. It was bad enough having fish sticks at school every Friday for four weeks but more at home midweek was too much, at least tonight. I had a few bites then ate just the macaroni and cheese.

"Not good enough for you?" Shirleen said.

Yolanda took my fish and I left the table. I called Dad collect. I was surprised he was home. He sounded sleepy. I asked if I would still come for summer or longer and he said yes. When I hung up I felt brokenhearted. I wanted him to come and get me that night, let Yolanda finish the school year and get her later. I felt guilty wanting to leave Yolanda so I helped her practice her spelling words before bed. Shirleen made me nervous, walking around and looking but hardly talking. I felt like I had to make something up to her but whatever it was, I wouldn't do it. I was the child and she owed me.

· · ·

We had Holy Thursday and Good Friday off from school and spent both days cleaning first Mother Dear's house then ours, swept sticky bits of web and cockroach wings from every corner, dusted every gritty cranny, washed dusty plates and glasses and dried them by hand so there would be no spots, washed and dried all the laundry, even bed sheets folded in the closet and never used. Holy Saturday Shirleen did our hair. I watched her hot comb, part and roll Yolanda's hair on a couple dozen pink sponge rollers. I hated sleeping on rollers for holidays. The sponge ones were softer than the wire-center ones but even the plastic rods and clasps dug into my scalp. The only way to sleep was on my stomach with my chin in the pillow to keep the rollers up. Then it was my turn. Shirleen said nothing. She pulled, tugged, scratched my scalp with the comb saying it was flaky but it only felt scraped and I could taste metal. When I said it hurt, she hit my head with the comb's teeth and told me to shut up. Yolanda winced.

"And I'm not sorry," Shirleen said. She pulled harder as she talked. "What am I supposed to tell people? What do I tell Mother Dear? I tell her you went to live with him and the first thing she'll say is, Can't keep your own daughter, huh? And no one will think you made some cockeyed decision, they'll think I did something wrong and I have not, no matter what you say. I do everything for you. I sacrificed everything for you. And all I get is shit!" she said and pushed my head so hard I almost fell out of the chair. She went to the bathroom, slamming the door. Since Dad called about my letter, because the living room, also her bedroom, had no door to slam, she had started stomping into the bathroom when she was mad.

Yolanda looked confused. "You're leaving?"

I blew my nose; it and my eyes had started to drip from feeling and hearing hairs snap in the comb. "We both are."

"To go where?"

"Dad. Wherever he is."

"He's not with Mama, is he?"

"No. And she'll never find out."

"I don't want to go," she said. "I want to stay here."

"With . . ." I nodded my head towards the bathroom.

"She's nice to me. And he's your dad."

"And she's my mom."

"That doesn't matter to her. And I like school. Next year I'll have Sister Joan," she said with a big smile.

I lay that night with my head propped up, wide awake. I didn't know if I was sad because Lydia was gone or Dad was gone or Mamalita was gone or Yolanda didn't want me or Shirleen hated me so. I couldn't understand why I cared if she hated me when I didn't like her anymore but it made me feel like no one could, would or did like me, like Sister Lawrence and Sister Paul hated me and were nice just to look like nice people. I wanted to talk to Sister Paul. She'd made Lydia feel better though I wasn't as bad off as Lydia. I alternately imagined Sister Paul hugging me tight while I cried and closing her office door in my face.

· · ·

The last week of school every class did a lot of art projects. I drew pictures of houses I'd seen when I'd visited Mamalita and flowers from Miss Alice's yard. Yolanda brought home dozens of coloring pages every day. She was happier than she'd ever been at school.

Yolanda passed all her subjects. Shirleen bought a cake. It had Happy Birthday in purple icing on top, a cake someone hadn't picked up and she got cheap after work, but it was moist chocolate with butter icing so sweet and thick it hurt the back of my throat.

The last day we got out before lunch. Yolanda gave some

of her coloring pages to Shirleen and kissed her on the cheek. When Shirleen looked at me, I knew she didn't want anything except me to say I would stay and though I'd lied to her about many other things, I couldn't tell that lie.

. . .

Shirleen woke me with a slap on the back of the legs. At the store the day before, she had filled the basket with party food—macaroni, three pounds of cheese, two ten-pound bags of potatoes, a jar of pickles, the biggest jar of mayonnaise the Schwegmann's had, three whole chickens, ribs, ground meat, potato chips.

"We having another party?" Yolanda said to her.

Shirleen cut her eyes at me before she answered Yolanda. "We always have a party at the end of the year. Besides, you're going to third grade!"

"We who?" I said. Shirleen's mouth had turned down.

Yolanda yawned. Before she could open her eyes, Shirleen said, "Go ahead and sleep, Yo. All I need is Sandi."

Shirleen was in her robe, dark legs showing each time she walked. I listened for groans, a deep voice, or water running in the bathroom but there was nothing. When I stepped to the bathroom to brush my teeth, Shirleen pushed me toward the kitchen. "Get the potatoes started first."

"I was gonna brush my teeth."

Once I had a big pot of water on the stove, I went into the living room to ask Shirleen something but mostly to see if her friend was gone or sleeping late. He was gone. Shirleen sat on the sofa, cutting her toenails and the room had the musty, sweaty smell it had after she had a friend over. I'd meant to ask Lydia what that was about, too. Shirleen didn't look up so I turned and went back to the kitchen, to the twenty pounds of potatoes I was in the middle of peeling. Next I had shrimp to clean, chicken to cut up, macaroni to boil, cheese to grate. I hated parties. Shirleen liked to ask why I was "always so down in the damn mouth" when she had a party and if she asked this time, I'd tell her—because I did all the work and I'm tired and I have no friends so what does a party mean to me?

The potatoes were peeled, chunked and in the pot of water, the flame under it high so that by the time they were ready, I'd have the chicken cut up for Shirleen to dip and bread. Next came the shrimp for jambalaya—I was guessing since Shirleen hadn't told me what it was for—cheese to grate and pickles and onions to cut for the potato salad. I had a schedule in my head of what I would do next so when Shirleen was ready to cook, everything she needed cleaned, boiled, chopped was at hand.

Yolanda came out of the bathroom fresh and clean and I could barely see her through onion tears. I was headed past her to the bathroom to rinse my face and finally brush my teeth when Shirleen's fingers clamped around my arm and snatched me back so hard, my head snapped and I felt like Philipa was about to push me down the stairs.

"Where the fuck do you think you're going?" Shirleen said.

"To brush my teeth," I said.

"Uuh, you ain't brushed your teeth yet?" Yolanda said, covering her nose with her hand.

"I have not been allowed to brush my teeth."

Shirleen slapped me on the back of the head. "Hit me one more time," I said before I could stop myself, "and I'm calling the police."

I was standing at the bathroom sink, finally brushing my teeth—I'd been cutting, cleaning, rinsing and peeling for more than three hours—and Shirleen kicked the door open and started smacking my bare legs with Sock It to Me. I straightened my back so I'd be firm on my feet and kept brushing. My skin felt pricked with needles and I was waiting for it to go numb. Shirleen stopped, stood behind me in the mirror her face twisted. "Don't you hear me talking to you?"

"You weren't talking, you were beating me."

"I'll show you what a beating is—"

"Why repeat yourself?" I walked out of the bathroom, expecting to feel her right behind me, heavy stomps vibrating the floor under my feet but she didn't. I wanted to throw the food on the floor but I wasn't going to be like Shirleen and punish other people for what she had done like she punished me for things I hadn't done.

When Yolanda came in the kitchen, I heard Shirleen tell her to go outside and play.

• • •

I heard deep and high voices in the living room and the screen door slammed at least five times. I got out the cast iron skillet and set up the bowls for the chicken—one with milk, the other with flour mixed with pepper and salt for the breading—but Shirleen still didn't come in. I had everything ready for her to come cook but she wasn't coming. For a minute I was confused—my schedule, my list broke apart in my head and all the pieces went flying and I had no idea what to do. I had to sit down to think—what took longest and should start cooking first, what was fastest, what had the most steps, what I could do while chicken fried.

Voices behind my back said hello, good work, hey girl while I mixed together the macaroni, cheese, milk and butter in the big baking pan with my hands like I'd seen Mamalita do. I left the shrimp in the bowl on the table.

"Shirl?" It was Aunt Margie. "What you gon' do with the shrimp?"

"She making jambalaya," Shirleen yelled from the backyard.

"She who? And does *she* know that?" Aunt Margie came up next to me, shaking her head. "All right, Sandrine, where should I jump in?"

Shirleen, who'd only walked through the kitchen all morning, never stopping, suddenly stood right behind us, talking loud like she was still in the yard. "Margie, get the hell out, she don't need no help."

"At ten years old she's gon' cook for all the fools you invited over here?"

"She ain't the first ten-year-old to cook dinner. She'd be done if her ass wasn't so lazy and contrary and just plain dumb."

The word hit my skin only. I felt Aunt Margie look at me but I kept dipping the chicken pieces into the milk with one hand and rolling them through the flour with the other, wondering if Shirleen or Mamalita used more than flour. "Shirl, that's just downright mean," Aunt Margie said. "She's always on the honor roll—"

"The Beta, not the Alpha."

"How many times were you on the honor roll?"

"I got all y'all ready for school, took y'all to school, cooked dinner, did laundry, cleaned the house, and went to PTA meetings, that's why I wasn't on no honor roll." She stomped back outside where the deep voices were.

Aunt Margie sighed deep and long two times. She checked the macaroni in the oven then gently touched my hand. I was surprised and put down the piece of chicken I was dipping. Aunt Margie smiled wide at me and started doing the chicken. "What else you have to do, hon?"

"Hamburgers and fry the chicken."

"We'll fry it when more folks get here . . . .Shirl told you that before?"

"That I'm dumb?"

She shook her head like she was trying to shake the word out her ears. "She ever tell you before how she got us all to school and met with teachers and cooked dinner every night?" I nodded. Aunt Margie sighed again and I wondered what was wrong with her. "Not a damn word is true," she said. I got the ground meat out of the refrigerator. Aunt Margie touched my hand again and I looked at her face. She looked so much like Shirleen, especially around the mouth and eyes, that at first I felt like I was too close to her to be safe. "Did you hear me? None of it's true." I thought she meant about me being dumb but something in my stomach started churning and I knew there was something else, something I wasn't hearing with my brain but with my body.

Aunt Margie opened the screen door. "Shirl! Come in here."

As Shirleen came in, Aunt Margie pointed at the counter where the chicken was and, hand on my shoulder, led me to my room. She told me to get clean clothes to wear and then followed me into the bathroom. She told me to draw a bath and get clean. She didn't leave and I felt my stomach turn that she was staying but when I started taking off my pajamas, she looked down at her nails until I was deep in the tub.

"Feel good?" she said.

"Yes." I soaped up a towel. Aunt Margie took the towel and scrubbed my back and it felt so good I closed my eyes and rested my head on my wet knees and it was the best I'd felt in a long time.

"Mother Dear told me you're going to live with your father for awhile," she said softly.

"She doesn't want me and I don't ..." I started crying without wanting to, without saying what I really felt, that I didn't want Shirleen anymore either. Aunt Margie slid the warm towel up and down my back and hummed a song about flying away home.

We ignored the first knock. The second knock was louder and longer and when Aunt Margie went to the door, I tried to cover up with the towel but instead of letting anyone in, she whispered then closed the door. A third knock made her open the door again but this person wouldn't back down.

"She'll be done in a few minutes."

"It's all right, I could come in, Shirl don't mind." Goose-bumps covered my body like the air coming in the ajar door was ice cold but it was the voice, Champ's voice. "She say the girl too damn slow anyhow."

"What kind of fool—oh, wait, I forgot we talking about my sister who must be a fool to tell some man she barely knows to go in the bathroom with her daughter naked in the tub." Champ's heh-heh laugh started and Aunt Margie slammed the door closed, cutting it off. "Yuck!" Aunt Margie said, twisting her arms up like a kid and making a face. I wanted to laugh but my skin felt so goosebumpy it was like someone else's skin. With Champ in the house, I wanted to stay in the bathroom the rest of the day. He was sure to stand close to me or say something to me or something to Shirleen that would make her eyes wide and hot, convinced—.

"Were my parents married?" I'd never asked anyone, Dad, Shirleen, Dear, any of my aunts or uncles anything about my mother or even their childhoods. I'd always had Shirleen's ver-sion—she cooked, cleaned, washed, mended, walked to school, helped with homework, did everything for them and then my father left her pregnant and I better not ask anybody else like she's lying. I watched Aunt Margie carefully for any downturn in the mouth or narrowing of the eyes.

Aunt Margie sighed again. I'd never noticed how much she sighed before. "Well . . . no."

"Because Dad wouldn't?"

"They couldn't. Mother Dear wouldn't let them. You know how old your mother was, huh?" I shook my head. Aunt Margie leaned back and instinctively looked over her shoulder though she only saw the wall over the toilet. "Shirl turned fifteen after you were born."

"She's only twenty-five?" I said so loudly I could hear my voice bounce off the walls.

"She's just about twenty-five."

"But she—how's she oldest?"

Aunt Margie laughed. "Carina in California is oldest. She's the one did all that. And that's also why we'll never see her again." I had heard Carina's name once or twice and never from Shirleen. "Let's get you out. If we don't hurry up out of here, your mama's trashy friends'll start pissing all over the place. Doesn't your mother have any female friends?"

Aunt Margie did my hair for me in my room, her on my bed, me on the floor between her knees. She told me that Mother Dear had been a very young mother, too, and when she got distracted, by a lost job, a new boyfriend, Ray Charles coming to the Dew Drop Inn or a new baby, Carina took over, made sure the little food they had was divided evenly, that everyone had clean clothes and actually got to school and sometimes she stole money from Mother Dear's purse or begged from neighbors, usually for food but sometimes to keep the lights and water on or pay for a lost book at school. When Dear finally found out Shirleen was pregnant—Aunt Margie said Shirleen was almost seven months pregnant before Dear noticed the weight gain and baggy clothes—Dear blamed Carina and beat her until she was black and blue and bloody. The next day, Carina was gone, all her clothes, everything left behind. Margie and Z got a letter a few months later and that was it. Margie called her on holidays. Sometimes Carina didn't answer.

"Black and blue?" I said, thinking of Margie's, Shirleen's and Z's dark chocolate skin. And then the picture on the console TV flashed into my mind, I could see it better than the floor in front of me and I knew who I'd thought was a white teacher or social worker wasn't white and wasn't some passer-by but the only picture of Carina I would ever see.

Aunt Margie shook her head and sighed. "She looked like she got hit by a truck." She kept shaking her head without saying more, finished my hair, a ponytail of braids, and I felt light in the head but heavy in the body, like Shirleen's lies were weighing me down.

By the time we got to the kitchen, Shirleen had four people helping her—Dear, Auntie Z, Cherry, and even Joe Henry at the table rubbing salt and pepper into the ribs. "Go do something fun," Aunt Margie whispered to me. When Shirleen looked behind her, forehead crunched up and mouth set, Aunt Margie stepped between us so Shirleen couldn't see me and I slipped into the living room for the portable radio Raheem usually brought to parties. I took it outside, going out the front door and through the alley, tuning to a station, smiling because I was going to be in the party, not just making it. I looked up before stepping into the yard and in the path was Champ. The taste and smell of vomit came to my mouth and I swallowed hard to keep it down. He smiled, one arm against the house, the other against the fence, blocking me in. Again. I saw bits of shirts, arms and legs behind him.

"Hey, girl, come give your uncle Champ a kiss."

I slammed the radio into his chin and tried to squeeze past under his arm by the fence. His arm clamped down on me, elbow digging into my waist. I pulled and tried to twist away but I was wedged between his arm and body and he smelled like something burned that got doused with beer. Then his hand touched my bare skin, his palm on the seat of my shorts, his fingers on my thigh and I screamed, grabbed the fence and tried to pull away from him. I thought I heard him laughing, took a breath and just as I started my second scream I felt a larger hand on my arm and Champ leaning away from me—Joe Henry pushed Champ one last time and pulled me free, squeezing my arm tight to keep me from falling over onto the ground.

"What the fuck is your problem?" Joe Henry said to Champ.

Raheem's green dashiki brushed my face as he reached down for the radio and clicked it off. "You all right there?" Raheem said. The scream had taken all my words. I nodded.

"Go flip some burgers for me," Joe Henry said to me or somebody, his eyes on Champ, but nobody moved.

"I was just kidding with her, bro," Champ said.

I saw Joe Henry's fist in Champ's chest and Champ stumbled backwards, his grab at the fence making it wobble and chime. As he backed up the alley to the street, Joe Henry kept pushing him in the chest with his fist. "Uh-oh," someone behind me said and I felt people right behind me as I went up the alley, too.

A screen door slammed and Shirleen appeared at the end of the alley, hands on hips. "Joe Henry!" He was still pushing Champ but Shirleen was now punching at Joe Henry's arm, her skinny fists effective on me but not even noticed by Joe Henry. "Leave him be, Joe Henry!" Shirleen said. "No fightin' in my house, no fightin' in my house!"

That made Joe Henry stop. He looked back at me. "Do you want him here?"

Champ smiled at me and pursed his lips in a kiss that

Shirleen noticed
I told her, I was
anything she said

Shirleen can
claws. Trying to
but Shirleen sna
concrete stairs. I
and I felt hands
Shirleen's grip o
hug—I smelled
the kitchen. Voi
instead I cried, n
but because Aun
ever see Carina a

. . .

Shirleen hadn't asked how I'd get there. I called a cab to take me
to the bus station. I put a book and a pack of cards with a change
of clothes and the can of money in the overnight case I'd keep
on the seat next to me. I gave Yolanda my Barbies and toys and
packed every book I had in a box I got from the store where I
got Joe Henry's newspapers.

Shirleen and Yolanda helped me carry the suitcases to the
cab. Yolanda squeezed me as tight as she could and promised
twice to write every weekend. I felt Shirleen looking at me so
I looked up. Her eyes were sad. She gave me a half-smile. "I do
love you, you know," she said. I hugged her tightly and at that
moment, I missed her. When I closed the cab door and saw her
walk into the house without looking back once, I didn't miss her
anymore. She didn't want me. And I had somewhere to go.

The last thing I saw through the back window was Yolanda
with a huge smile, waving her hands wildly.

3

Every face in the waiting room or leaning over the wood counter of the nurses' station or peeking out of rooms in the hall had a big smile directed at me. The square waiting room had a bench and several different chairs, some solid wood chairs, others with wood plank or basket-weave seats, plastic molded chairs in faded orange and teal, and two knee-high rocking chairs in the corner near a pile of plastic cars and naked dolls. The people sitting in the waiting room I guessed were patients and even they smiled at me—a dark-skinned old man leaning on a rubber-tipped cane; a girl maybe a few years older than Lydia with caramel skin, a fat baby on one knee who drooled around the finger in its mouth, a toddler sitting on the floor between her feet; an older woman in a flower print dress with pale skin and black eyes and hair. The people in the hall and behind the counter all wore white, either uniforms or lab coats, most were women and when I heard the glass door seep closed behind Dad, I realized every single face was black, not just one or two shades of dark or medium brown but every shade, even mine.

"If she don't look like Dr. Miller . . ." The nurse behind the counter shook her head and smiled even wider. "Come over here and let me get a look at you."

She told me her name was Cheryl Brock and to call her Miss C or Nurse C, like the kids did. Dad said she was a pediatric nurse but did a little of everything there, like all the staff did. I met the other nurses—Kiswana and Mattie—who looked at me then batted their eyes at my dad. As he and I were leaving the nurses' station to show me off down the hall, I heard Kiswana say, "Damn if it don't look like he spit her out," and another answer, "You know that's right." Down the hall was another doctor, a medium-skinned woman with an Afro and a strong handshake, Dr. June she told me to call her before she disappeared back into the exam room she'd popped out of. At the end of the hall was a small pharmacy and a small lab. The pharmacist leaned over the Dutch door to take my hands in his and said, "Welcome" and I realized Mr. Pradeesh wasn't black but Indian, his skin as dark as Dr. June's, his nose wide and flat like mine. I was still looking back at him when I heard a squeal like eighth grade girls meeting up again after summer vacation. I was hugged before I realized who was hugging me—Miss Frances, the head of the lab that was just a little bigger than the nurses' station, and her assistant, Mrs. Feydeau. They drowned me in magnolia perfume that clung to me all day, thick lipstick kisses on my cheek, and squeezes of my shoulders once the long tight hugs were over. Miss Frances had light skin like me and a curly Afro and wore a dashiki under her lab coat. Mrs. Feydeau wore a plain blue dress and old walking shoes with her lab coat. "Oooh," Mrs. Feydeau said, her brown face wrinkled up in a smile, "She's so cute you just want to eat her up. Now when you gon' come help us back here?"

"Dr. Miller makes it sound like you're ready for med school tomorrow," Miss Frances said and she and Mrs. Feydeau broke out in giggles. They waved as Dad and I went back up the hall and I could hear their voices chirping back and forth and giggling. Dr. June left one exam room, caught my father's eye and smiled. "I'll take it, you get her settled," she said before taking the chart on the door and going in. Kiswana peeked out of the door of the nurses' station. I had seen women with braids like hers on TV a few times, a head full of thin smooth braids with colored beads and what looked like little seashells on the ends, and it made me think about my own hair, Mamalita cornrowing it, and then a sad memory of Lydia gently braiding my hair.

"Doc?" Kiswana said. "You're not going to leave her in that house by herself, are you?"

"She could stay here." It was Nurse C's voice. "Lord knows we could use the help."

"Oh, uh-uh, we get her first," called Mrs. Feydeau and she and Miss Frances laughed out loud.

"All right, ladies, let's not put her to work yet," Dad said, a big smile on his face. "This is my office," he said. "Anytime you need to get away from the hens, you hide yourself in here."

The office was a little smaller than my bedroom in New Orleans, with one window like my room had had. It had one big metal filing cabinet, a desk stacked with papers and books and what looked like miniature phone books, three molded plastic chairs, an end table with an electric percolator on top, and right next to the desk a toppled pile of files in manila folders with big color-coded letters on the edges. It smelled like rubbing alcohol and the full ashtray on the windowsill. Behind the desk and under the window was a small Army cot, a folded lab jacket as pillow and greenish paper like they put over the exam tables half-on and half-off the cot. Dad showed me the bathroom off to the side—narrow but with a sink, toilet and even a shower stall. He told me to clean up if I wanted, left his car keys for me if I wanted clothes out of my suitcase in the trunk, and said I was free to go anywhere except Dr. June's office and occupied exam rooms. Then he went out the door and even with the rustle of people walking outside and voices coming through the thin paneled walls and doors, I felt silent and alone.

. . .

Dad had been surprised when only I got off the bus, looking behind me for Yolanda, but only his eyes showed surprise. He had brought me some food—a Styrofoam container full of fried chicken, cole slaw, potato salad, an ear of corn and two slices of white bread at the bottom tan from chicken breading and grease. He said he'd have to take me to the clinic but that that was good because I'd get to meet everybody, they had all been waiting and asking when I was due.

Five minutes away from the bus station, there was nothing but cotton, corn, cows, horses, houses and barns with weathered brown wood, trailers, little whitewashed churches, but mostly trees—pine, pecan, oak, more pine. Dad had another car, a blue Thunderbird with a white vinyl top. Eating made me even lighter-headed and more tired and the blur of green from leaves, grass and crops plus the swish as the car passed trees and fences of wood stakes and barbed wire hypnotized me; my eyes were open but I felt asleep.

We drove almost an hour to get to the clinic and I'd been surprised—I'd expected a two-story brick building like a doctor's office in New Orleans but instead we'd pulled onto a dirt road and slid to a stop next to what looked like a wide shotgun house surrounded by trees. One old car and a few newer ones had been parked on the other side of the building and in the back stood a horse, watching Dad and me carefully with one eye and then the other as we got out of the car and walked to the building.

I pushed the ashtray aside and lay my head on my hands on the sill. The shade from the trees cooled the breeze as it came in. I could tell this was not a place where doctors got rich; Shirleen would never believe it.

. . .

When I woke up it was just light, still grayish so I knew it was early. I had been dreaming I still had my head on the windowsill, watching the horse weave its head from side to side to look at me with one eye and then the other, and was surprised to open my eyes to blue-flecked wallpaper, a closet door, three windows with thin curtains that lifted up and down slightly like someone gently blowing them. I smelled coffee then I smelled bacon. I sat up. Dad had said the day before, Dr. June and Nurse C nodding in the background with serious faces, that his house was too far away for me to stay alone so I'd be with him at the clinic most of the time. I threw open my suitcase to get a sundress that was comfortable but not a church one.

Outside the room was a long dim hall, a worn carpet down the center. I opened each door on each side, Dad's room which I could tell from the smell of smoke and the pants draped over the closet door, one empty room and at the end a wide high-ceilinged bathroom. Every room looked old but taken care of, like the girl's dress in *The Hundred Dresses*—old and worn but clean and neat. It was a little humid and smelled like Dad's after shave. When I finished, it was cooler and smelled like Pepsodent and hair oil.

We had scrambled eggs, bacon, toast and jelly for breakfast then I helped Dad make a pile of ham sandwiches, one with mustard, one with mayonnaise and three for him with mustard, mayonnaise and horseradish spread thick on the bread. He went to the door and I ran to put things away before he left me—

Shirleen each Sunday simply went to the door without telling me she was ready for church and I had to rush to put things away and get shoes—but he came in relaxed and smiling with a big pickle jar of sun tea. While he got his lab coat and cigarettes, I stirred sugar into the tea and put it and the bag of sandwiches in the back seat. Dad told me to get some shorts and a t-shirt for playing outside, said I might be able to get in on a game of rope or marbles with some kids waiting for younger siblings or grandparents they'd walked with or driven to the clinic. I thought he was kidding but he said even he had learned to drive at thirteen—in the country, you needed to know how to drive a tractor or a truck for all kinds of reasons, much less emergencies. I guessed I'd be able to stay at the house alone if I knew how to drive but as we drove away, I realized I didn't want to be there alone. The house was small and squat, wood unpainted and gray-brown from rain and sun except for the window frames painted stained-glass green. The porch along the front was dotted with rusted kitchen chairs. The land around the house was four times the size of the house and a weathered barn toward the back of the plot looked the size of Shirleen's shotgun plus Dear's shotgun and yard and the neighbor on the other side of Dear. I felt scared just looking back at it. We drove a long time before I saw another house and it was just a trailer, the door open, no stairs; it looked empty. I felt dizzy thinking about now, thinking about New Orleans, and what Shirleen would say or do, translating everything from what I knew to what was my new now.

• • •

I spent the rest of the week filing. I started in Dad's office, with the collapsed stack next to his desk. Mattie peeked in every ten minutes to ask how I was doing until I heard Kiswana say, "She's doing a better job than you so leave her be." It took time because when I thought I had found the right place in the files, I'd see that other things were misfiled but by the end of the day, I finished. Nurse C and Kiswana had me in the nurses' station the next day, filing patient records in the open shelves on the walls. My hands got dry and papery but it was better than raw from ammonia or washing clean dishes to put back in cabinets.

The clinic was full most of the morning. Kiswana, Mattie or Nurse C stayed in the nurses' station unless all the exam rooms and chairs in the waiting room were full and they'd all leave to help. In the waiting room were old men and women, girls with babies, kids of all ages. Babies sick or getting shots cried off and on. Once Kiswana heard me answer the phone, saying "Benita Clinic" in the same light voice I'd heard them use, she and Mattie didn't double back when the phone rang; Mattie showed me the hold button and the appointment book so I could write people in while she and Kiswana fetched people from the waiting room or helped in back.

"New receptionist, ladies?" Mrs. Feydeau stood in the nurses' station doorway, arms folded, a sweet smile on her face. Kiswana and Mattie, both in the station for the first time since that morning, looked at each other then at me. Mattie laughed.

"She's so good we forgot," she said.

"Then she could come—"

"Lunch break!" Kiswana said. She took a sandwich wrapped in wax paper and the iced tea out of the refrigerator in the corner. "Get some fresh air." Even Mrs. Feydeau, who I knew was older than Kiswana no matter how sweet her face, obeyed Kiswana. She had the kind of voice you listened to, like Sister Mary Clare. Mrs. Feydeau went to wash out a cup for me.

The waiting room was almost empty, just a very large, very dark woman sitting in one of the plastic chairs, her hips touching the chairs on either side. She lurched forward twice like she was going to get up then leaned back again. Kiswana and Mattie talked quietly then Mattie leaned over the counter. "Dr. Capdeau'll be ready for you in a few minutes," she said to the woman.

"Capdeau? . . . Which one that?" the woman said, taking deep ragged breaths. With the waiting room empty the air conditioner had cooled things off but she still sweated on her forehead and neck.

Kiswana took a deep breath, straightened her back and turned away but I could see her face set and mad.

"Dr. Joan Capdeau," Mattie said.

"No, let me see . . . the man."

"Every damn time," Kiswana said. "She doesn't like women doctors, she doesn't like 'nappy headed women,' she only comes here because the white doctor is too far away and charges too much. She told me to go comb my hair." She shuddered so hard the shells in her hair tinkled. "That woman raises my blood pressure."

I almost lost my appetite thinking about the woman wanting my dad because he was as close to a white doctor as she could afford. It made me think about school, about a cinnamon girl who passed me in the hall while I was looking at the honor rolls and spit at me, "You still not white." But she was gone by the time I answered, "I never said I was." The only white people I talked to were at school and at stores when Shirleen wanted me to get a saleswoman's attention. And when I brought the saleswoman over to Shirleen, the woman's face would drop and her smile get mannequin stiff. I shook my head. If I thought any longer, my appetite would disappear completely.

"Go eat," Nurse C said. "You look pale." I checked her face to see if she meant anything by it but she only looked concerned.

I ate outside. Two girls stood near the front door, hands

behind their backs, sneaking looks at me as I sat on the packed dirt next to the clinic, under the pecan trees. Both were dark with several stiff braids sticking out at all angles, no rubber bands, ponyknots or holders. One wore cutoffs, the other a faded dress that ended mid-thigh. Neither wore shoes. The girl in cutoffs jingled something in her pocket then whispered to the other girl who looked at me with wide eyes. The girl in cutoffs sucked her teeth at the one in the dress and walked closer to me but stayed a few feet back, like I might be dangerous.

"You come here sick?" she said.

"No, my dad works in there."

She turned back and poked her tongue out at the girl in the dress. She came a few steps closer and took a small blue ball out of her pocket. "I tol' her you was prob'ly kin to somebody in there . . . What your name?"

"Sandrine."

"Sandrine?" A crick I had in my neck from earlier in the week flared up and sharp pain shot through my shoulder and neck while I waited for her to call it confusing or stupid or shorten it to something without my consent. "That's pretty. Her name Sandrine," she said over her shoulder to the other girl. She dropped to her knees and emptied her pocket—plain metal jacks and another ball, this one red. "You know how to play jacks?"

I didn't want her to know I hadn't played before but if I lied, as soon as the ball bounced the first time, I knew she'd be able to tell. "A little bit," I said.

"It's easy. Ain't no score or nothing. Susie!"

Susie walked over very slowly, carefully placing down each foot, and wrapped her dress around her thighs before she knelt so close to the cutoffs girl their braids poked each other. The cutoffs girl screwed up her face and shoved Susie with her elbow. "Move, now, you all in my damn lap."

They gave me extra turns to get onesies and twosies. We looked up a few times, at cars or a pickup truck passing and by the second game, I was good enough to not slow them down too much but Susie and the cutoffs girl played like lightning, the ball and their hands a blur. Then I saw Dad leaning out his office window. I jumped and felt like I had no air but Dad just smiled and went back in. I waited for him to come out the clinic door, order me back inside but he never came out, just a woman with three little kids then two very old people, the woman helping the man into the driver's side of their old Ford truck.

Susie said she wanted to play hopscotch. The cutoffs girl started drawing a hopscotch in the dirt, a kind I'd never seen, and we were searching for the right rocks when a woman, tall as my dad and as dark as he was light, stepped out of the clinic. The purse she carried looked more like an overnight bag and too heavy for her skinny arms to lift. She shrugged the thin green sweater off her shoulders and took out a white handkerchief. "Susie Lee, Dessa," she said evenly and then just waited, no yelling, no hurry up, no glares or threats. Susie silently shuffled away but Dessa lingered to pick up and blow off each jack before putting it in her pocket.

"You go to school?" Dessa said.

"I will."

She nodded and walked away. The three of them walked up the road. Dessa turned back to wave at me before they passed out of sight behind trees. Though I didn't think Susie liked me much, Dessa hadn't made fun of my name, called me yellow, snatched the ball out of my hand because I was too slow or thought that I didn't know how to play hopscotch. And I missed Yolanda, alone in the house, I knew, or cleaning Dear's house, watching too much TV, not even waiting for someone to get her, settled in with Shirleen.

The waiting room was empty and all the exam room doors were open. I peeked into the last one—Kiswana wiped off the padded exam table and put a new green paper sheet over it. She smiled back at me. "Have fun playing with Dessa?" She washed up to her elbows at the tiny sink and looked me up and down while drying her hands. "Doctor Miller do your hair?"

I laughed. "No, me."

Her eyes wrinkled into a smile. "Then you do a damn fine job," she said and walked out past me.

• • •

The clinic was supposed to be closed on Saturdays but Dad and Kiswana opened it, unofficially, until lunch time. Kiswana had a house out in the country, too, where one of her grandparents had lived and on Saturday mornings she would bring us something—collard greens, green onions, field peas, bags of crookneck squash. I knew how to cook collard greens but the squash got soft faster than I thought it would and ended up mushy.

My first Saturday at the clinic, no one came all morning and the clinic was quiet, just sighs and hisses from the refrigerators and scrapes as Dad lit cigarettes in his office. The next Saturday three people were waiting at the door when we got there but within an hour, it was quiet again. I found a broom in a supply closet and was sweeping the waiting room when Kiswana drove her yellow VW Beetle away, I thought to go home, but she came back twenty minutes later with Dessa who jumped out of the car with a big smile.

My whole life no adult had ever brought me a playmate.

• • •

When I got tired of filing, writing appointments, and shaking test tubes, I read in Dad's office. Kiswana had given me some shorts, t-shirts, a pair of green Converse one size too big that I wore every day anyway, and piles of books, biographies of black Americans, books about Swahili and of African folktales, and books I'd read before like *A Hero Ain't Nothin' But a Sandwich* and Langston Hughes' poems and *Simple* stories. Mixed in was a paperback about a runaway; the back cover said she got mixed up in drugs, violent friends, stealing. I threw the book back in the bag.

That night I dreamed I was walking down the dirt road that led to the clinic, one side of the road lined with cars instead of trees. I could barely feel my feet touch the ground and my chest felt too light, like I'd been filled with helium. A rumbling made me step to the side of the road and from behind me came a too-long red car, the engine sounding like a house-sized tractor. I didn't want to look but did. The man driving had skin like pine bark and where his eyes should've been were black circles of night sky without stars. I opened my mouth to scream but what came out sounded like cooing pigeons. As the car drove away, Lydia leaned out of the back window, out of the car up to her waist, hair fluttering around her head.

I was on my feet at the bedroom door. The room was dim but not dark anymore and the air felt moist and cool. My chest hurt, like the dream screams were trapped inside.

My door opened a little and Dad's head popped in. "What happened?" he yawned.

I felt ashamed I'd woken him up; he worked so hard that every night before I went to sleep I checked for him in the living room, where I'd find him asleep on the sofa, colored gray by snow on the black and white TV, or in his room sprawled across the bed fully dressed. And tears filled my eyes because I thought I had no business being there giving Dad more to do. I wanted to hide under the bed.

"Get a little more sleep," he said. Dad tucked me in like I wasn't old enough for school yet and kissed my forehead.

When I woke the sun was bright and strong, the house quiet and I almost cried, sure Dad was gone and I was alone. I wanted to look out the windows for his car but didn't want to feel the disappointment when I didn't see it there. Instead I got myself ready for the day, cleaned the bathtub, sink and mirror after I was done, and slowly went down the hall.

The kitchen door was open and I smelled cigarette smoke. Dad waited for me on the kitchen stairs.

• • •

I looked through Dad's office for paper, finally found a blank legal pad and started a letter to Sister Paul. As I wrote Sister Paul's name, in my head I saw Sister Lawrence with her habit billowing and the rosary case in her hand and I wished I could feel her arm around me.

> Dear Sister Paul,
>
> I will not be going to St. John's this year because I moved in with my father in Mississippi. Yolanda is still there with my mother and you will see her next year. She is excited about third grade. I hope she does okay. I do not know what school I will go to yet but I have been reading a lot. A nurse who works with my dad gave me a lot of good books to read.
>
> Thank you, Sister Paul for all the prayer books. Please also tell Sister Lawrence thank you for the rosary she gave me. I cannot remember if I ever said thank you and I keep the rosary safe by my bed. If I ever come back to New Orleans, I will come by St. John's to say hello.
>
> Sister Paul, have you heard anything about Lydia?

Did you know that she ran away? I was hoping she wasn't really gone. Have you seen her? Has she written you? I want to write a letter to her house but her mother didn't like me and I think she would throw away letters from me. I just want to know that she is okay.

Thank you, Sister Paul.

I signed my name. I started copying it out neatly and wanted to add things, like why I wasn't living with Shirleen anymore but I thought Sister Paul might call Shirleen into her office and ask what happened, like she did with Lydia's mother. And it made me too dizzy to write that Lydia's mother didn't like me because I was black. I addressed an envelope and then sat the letter up against the lamp on Dad's desk because I wasn't sure what to do next out in the country. I had yet to see a blue mailbox, much less a corner for the box to sit on, and the mail got delivered by a man in his own car with a postal sticker on his back windshield.

I ate lunch outside. Kiswana came out after awhile, set a green paper sheet on the ground and sat near me. She had her own sandwiches and two bottles of Coke. "I need my afternoon second wind," she said with a smile. We ate awhile in silence. No cars or trucks passed though far away I could hear a tractor. I kept waiting for her to ask me something or say something but she didn't. We just chewed, drank, looked up at the leaves in the trees. It was hot even on the ground in the shade.

"Girls around here get pregnant early," Kiswana said. She turned to watch a few people go in the clinic and she sat a moment, maybe thinking she should go in to help. With her head half turned, the shells and beads spread across her shoulder, I wanted to touch them, they looked so perfect and unreal. "It's not boys you have to watch out for," she went on. "It's grown men two, three times your age."

"I know about that already."

Kiswana drank Coke, her eyes on me. "What do you know about it?"

"Are you from Mississippi?"

"Born and bred," she smiled. "I went away for school, though, to my aunt's in Chicago. And now I am here, serving my people."

"If y'all done with your picnic," Mattie called from the front door, "we could use some help up in here."

• • •

I heard a deep whisper but thought it was a dream though all I saw was the dark of half-sleep. Tires scraped over gravel then there was a deep silence that pulled my eyes open.

I got up, my head and arms heavy, to look in Dad's room. The bed was unmade, he was not in it, no other lights in the house were on. I thought I was dreaming until I saw a note taped to my door—an emergency, he'd be back when he could. I was awake then.

Not sure what to do with myself, I went back to my room and sat up in bed. I picked up one of the books on the floor by the bed but there wasn't enough light to read; unlike in New Orleans, there were no streetlights and if there was moonlight, it wasn't strong enough to reach all the way to the far side of the room where my bed was. The overhead light made my eyes hurt and I blinked and blinked until I could squint. Creaks and crackles came from the walls and floors all over the house, it sounded like, and my hands started shaking. I remembered Shirleen telling me Dad would leave me alone all the time, just like in Meridian, day and night. But Shirleen had left me alone day and night, too—I walked to school alone, I studied alone, I cleaned the house alone, when the girls didn't talk to me at school I was alone, when Yolanda came Shirleen turned what niceness she had onto her and cut me out, and when I left she turned away and didn't look back. I didn't think I'd hear from Shirleen; she probably thought I needed to learn a lesson about loyalty, who wanted me and who didn't.

As the sun came up, I was still awake but scratchy-eyed and heavy in the chest. I took a long bath. I held my face in the water to cool my eyes but imagined the man from my dream with no eyes staring down at me from the ceiling and got a chill down my back. I flipped water everywhere jumping out of the tub and drying myself fast, not looking at the ceiling because even though I knew he couldn't be there, I didn't want to look.

After I turned off lights, I went onto the front porch, the first time I'd gone out alone. Behind the house, in the fields, I heard machinery but even if I had stood in the middle of the lawn, I couldn't be seen through the trees and scraggy bushes that divided the house's plot from the rented fields. Along the front porch the dirt was dug up, lumps of clay soil so dry it looked orange streaked with pink. I thought about the books I'd been reading. Every person was good at something—speaking, writing, tracking her way through the woods, flying, running, tennis, basketball, baseball, medicine, inventions, dancing, painting. I tried to list in my mind what I was good at. I was good at getting As. I was good at cleaning. I sat and sat, the sun getting hotter, the shade losing its coolness and the sunlight edging across the porch closer and closer to me, the white clouds thinner and further apart until the sky was clear blue, birds flew in and out of the trees, my stomach grumbled louder and louder. My mind went blank and my empty stomach felt full. I wasn't good at anything.

Dad came back around lunch time, shoulders heavy, looking hollow-eyed and tired but he gave me a big smile and a tight hug before he went to his room. When I looked in later, he was sound asleep across his bed, shoes still on. I tiptoed in—I had learned all the creaks in his floor from the door to his bed and could get in and out without a sound—and took his shoes off for him. I turned the fan so it blew right at his face to cool him off.

I hadn't been in the house much in the heat of the day. The only cool place was on the kitchen linoleum with the screen door open and even there I felt damp with sweat but at least I wasn't dripping. From the bag Kiswana gave me, I had only skipped a few books so far that I'd already read. I lined all the books up and put them in alphabetical order by author last name. Then title. Then year of publication. Then I made a paperback bridge. A few flies bobbed up and down and in and out of the doorway. I wished the phone would ring though it rarely did and I didn't know who might call. I had no list of chores, no homework, no one to watch, no library to walk to, no kids to watch from windows. I could wait an hour and still not see a car or truck pass.

The later Dad slept, I realized we weren't going to the clinic. I got the legal pad I'd brought home from Dad's office. I wrote "Dear Lydia" then snatched off the sheet and tore it into confetti. I wrote "Dear Shirleen" and had to start again with "Dear Mom." I got some iced tea out of the refrigerator. We didn't have much food left, enough milk for cereal but no cereal, bacon and ham, one egg, a small container of potato salad that had been there since I came and that I was afraid to open. I wiped the sweat off the glass with a dish towel and pressed the cool spot on the towel to my forehead.

Dear Mama,

How are you? I am doing fine. Dad has a little house in the country. I go to work with him and help out. I do some filing, answer the phone if everybody is busy and Mrs. Feydeau lets me shake test tubes. One of the nurses gave me some books to read. I read about Madame C. J. Walker who became the first black woman millionaire. I also read a Louis Armstrong autobiography that was really funny but sad, too, because so many people where he grew up were so poor. New Orleans was more dangerous then.

How is Yolanda? I hope she is still excited about third grade. I wrote to Sister Paul last week but I have not gotten a letter back. Could you ask Yolanda to write me? I met a couple of girls but most of the kids who come to the clinic are a lot younger and sick, too. I would like to hear from Yolanda.

Dad had to go to an emergency last night. But don't worry. I am safe out here. I wonder how I will get to and from school when it starts. Do you think school busses go this far out to pick kids up? I can't imagine anyone walking to school out here.

I am safe and well. I hope you and Yolanda and Dear are, too.

I signed my name. I had folded it into fourths when I thought to go back and write "Love" above my name. I hadn't asked her to save letters for me. I didn't know if I should.

• • •

Another quiet Saturday. I heard Dad muttering to himself and dropping piles of file folders on his desk, the file cabinets squeaking open and soft powdery hissing as he sprayed WD-40 on the drawers. Kiswana I couldn't hear but she was going from exam room to exam room, checking supplies, wiping counters, getting them ready for the week. There was nothing to file or shake and I had been reading so much I expected people to speak in paragraphs and each doorway to be like a page turned, a new world or new chance to be had.

After they locked the door, Kiswana followed Dad and me into town to the Piggly Wiggly; every other Saturday she came with us to look in our cart and shake her head. "One of you needs to learn how to cook," she'd say, looking at the cans of Spaghettio's and creamed corn and bags of potato chips.

Kiswana held a jar of Peter Pan over the cart. "I don't like peanut butter," I said.

"You need some protein," Kiswana said. I looked up for Dad but he was still at the meat counter.

"Meat is protein."

"Meat is not the only protein. Smooth or crunchy?"

I followed Kiswana to the cereal aisle and while I put in boxes of Cocoa Pebbles and Honeycomb, cereal Shirleen never bought and that Dad let me get as much of as I could eat, Kiswana put grits and oats in the basket. She wasn't giving up and I felt a little frustrated but I also wanted to smile because she cared about what I ate. I wanted to have dreams that Kiswana was my mother but since the dream about the man with no eyes, I had stopped dreaming.

• • •

I was eating lunch and reading a history book with small, smeary print, looked up a little to get my cup of iced tea and saw bare feet. Dessa sat down in the dirt next to me. At least two, sometimes three times a week I'd look up from my lunch or look out a clinic window and see Dessa coming. When she wasn't looking, I marveled at how her head didn't jerk each time the clinic door opened or a car approached on the road, how she didn't seem to care I was paler or that my father was a doctor or that I seemed to have no mother and came from nowhere.

"Hi."

"Hey," she said. "I wait 'til you finish." She cocked her head to see the cover of the book. "You likin' that book?"

"Mostly." I ate another bite then put the book down. "Not mostly." I looked back at the clinic. "I'm kind of tired of history and biographies and speeches. I think the last book I read did it."

Dessa sat up straighter. "Did what?"

I caught myself thinking Dessa wouldn't understand any way I explained and felt so guilty I wanted to give her my lunch and everything I had, which wasn't much compensation. "Kiswana gave me one last week I didn't like too much. I mean, I liked it until he started talking about how evil black women are and how it's all their fault black men can't get anywhere in the world. He sounded like a boy saying all girls have cooties."

Dessa laughed and I felt better. "Yeah, don't sound right to me neither." She looked around. It was a hot but quiet day. It didn't feel as hot as in New Orleans; Dad said it was drier here so it felt less oppressive.

"And it made me mad 'cause what about the men who . . . I guess you don't have that here," I said.

Dessa stopped digging in her cutoffs pocket. Maybe it was coincidence but she always seemed to wear that pair of cutoffs and faded gray t-shirt. "What?"

"You don't walk to school so . . . every once in a while, a car would stop or follow us, some man trying to get us in the car or saying we pretty or stupid stuff like that."

Dessa smiled. "Naw, they just come to the house out here." She saw something on my face and said, "Susie? There's a man would wait outside school and she sit in the car with him 'til it's time for the bus to go. She ain't even fifteen yet. Great-gran said she gon' end up pregnant before high school if she don't get away from him."

"Yuck," I said. "How old is he?"

Dessa shrugged. And just like that, she pulled the jacks out of her pocket and set up for a game. I kept thinking about Susie sitting in a car in front of a school, her head down while a man talked soft and quiet next to her.

"I'd never do that," I said. Dessa looked up and tossed me the ball. "Sit in a car with a man like that. He could drive off with you."

Dessa smiled. "Me neither. But I think Susie might like it."

I shook my head. When I went in for pickup sticks, a surprise from Mrs. Feydeau, the first pickup sticks I'd ever had, I wanted to ask Dessa if she'd ever gotten in a car with a man or with that man or if she knew what would happen if she did but Dessa clapped when she saw the pickup sticks and all she wanted to do was play.

• • •

Kiswana drove her Beetle up the dirt and gravel driveway so slowly I could reach out and pull individual leaves off trees. The roots of my hair had gotten so thick I had given up pulling the half-matted roots apart to make braids. After a week of my hair pulled into lopsided buns and a day that I just wrapped it in a faded green bandana I'd found in a closet at the house, Kiswana told me to get in the car. I wasn't sure whose house we were going to and the bottom of my stomach felt uneasy but as we got closer to the house, I recognized the girl in the front yard feeding the chickens that wandered around a rusted propane tank off to the side—Dessa. The house looked a little like ours, weathered wood and a low front porch, but smaller. Dessa's great-grandmother appeared at the open front door and waved. While Kiswana talked to Dessa's great-grandmother, I helped Dessa finish feeding the chickens; we had to leave food under a few bushes off by the trees because Dessa said some of the chickens were half-wild and wouldn't come close enough to get feed from her. Susie sat on the back stairs outside the kitchen shelling peas. She didn't raise her head, only shifted her eyes to see Dessa and me, and kept her head hung low, like she was punished.

"Thank you, ma'am," Kiswana said. "Sandrine, Miss Bettie says she'll press your hair so you can at least do something with it. I'll pick you up later." She patted my shoulder, hopped into the Beetle and disappeared into the trees.

Miss Bettie still stood in the open doorway, now with one hand on her hip and a smile that wrinkled up her whole face. She was probably the oldest person I had met, aside from some very old people who came into the clinic. She was older than Mamalita had been or Dear was now, since Dear had started having kids before she finished high school. "Let me get the hot comb ready," Miss Bettie said and her voice was light and friendly and I smiled back. She moved slowly but without hesitation or fear, like slow was her way even before she got old.

Dessa started unbraiding her hair. "She'll prob'ly do mines, too, while she at it."

Miss Bettie found a pack of cards and sat me at the table with Dessa while she hot combed my hair. The inside of their house was dim, not much light coming in the small windows and in the kitchen, just one bulb hung from the ceiling. The bathroom was attached to the kitchen, like it was added on at the last minute. Their stove was older than Mamalita's had been and in the big room off the kitchen where Susie and Dessa slept on a mattress and Miss Bettie had a narrow cast-iron bed was a potbelly stove they must've used in winter. From my place at the table I could see the garment rack with all their clothes in the corner of the big room. There weren't many Dessa's size so I guessed I saw her in the cutoffs and t-shirt so much to save her other clothes for school; Shirleen often said she was thankful I had uniforms so she had fewer clothes to buy. Miss Bettie said nothing to Susie on the stairs in the open back door and Susie never stopped her very slow shelling.

Miss Bettie took a long time with my hair because she moved slow and even when it didn't hurt, she apologized for tugging or pulling. She got the hot comb close to my ear but never touched it with the comb; I had tough places at the tops of both ears from years of burns when Shirleen wasn't looking or was talking on the phone. After our third game of War, Dessa looked up to see how it was going and once Miss Bettie started braiding, I taught Dessa double solitaire and we played until Miss Bettie had finished cornrowing my hair. After sweating under my dense hair and the hot comb, I could feel cooler air on my scalp between the braids and air on my neck. Dessa and I switched chairs but it took Miss Bettie no time to do Dessa's hair; Miss Bettie did what she called a light press on Dessa and cornrowed her hair in the same pattern as mine.

We heard a tractor close by and Dessa and I went out. Instead of a tractor coming up the driveway it was Kiswana's Beetle. On her way inside, Susie flicked her eyes at me, looking me up and down, and then slowly closed her eyes and went inside. A clump of dirt shattered on the door after her. Dessa clapped her hands clean, looked at me a second then looked away "She's such a witch with a B," she said. Kiswana waved for me to get in as she circled in the orangish dirt in front of the house. Dessa threw her arms around me in a quick hug then ran inside.

The Rap Brown book I'd left on the passenger seat was still there, the bookmark Lydia's note, softer and grayer, more pinpoint holes in the folds but all the words and pictures still sharp. I only had to touch it to remember it all. I took it out just as Kiswana pulled her car in front of the clinic and the noisy engine cut off. When we got to the door, I held it out to her.

"Is this right?" I said.

Kiswana gently opened the pages and her eyebrows shot up. "Who gave you this?"

I held the door open for her, instantly chilled by a wave of cold air. "A girl at school."

Dad came out of his office and she quickly dropped the note inside her shirt.

"Speaking of school," she said to him, stopping him in his tracks, "what county is the girl in? Or you sending her to St. Martin's?"

"Hell no," he said then went down the hall into the lab.

"At least he's got ideas," Kiswana said. She patted her shirt. "We'll talk about this later."

· · ·

Grass tickled my legs as I walked to the mailbox at the road. I brought all the envelopes in and left them on the table until after dinner—Mrs. Feydeau had brought us a pot of black-eyed peas—and even then I looked at the envelope for me a long time before I opened it. The handwriting was perfect, like in a handwriting book—Sister Paul. When I unfolded her letter, a prayer booklet and two saint bookmarks fell out.

Dear Sandrine,

I am so happy to hear that you are doing well. We here are preparing for the new school year. You are probably surprised to hear we work all summer long!

Yes, Yolanda should be excited about third grade. With your help, she ended the year with solid grades and should not need as much extra help. Your classmates will miss you in seventh grade, I am sure.

Have you been attending Mass? The nearest Catholic church to you, Father MacNeeley tells me, is St. Martin de Porres. I do not know the priests there but I am sure you will be able to continue your catechism and be confirmed next year. Please let the priests know that if they need any information, they can contact me here at the school.

I have not heard from Lydia Petitjean. Her brothers think she is with relatives in Texas but it is a branch of the family (on Mrs. Petitjean's side, I think) with whom they have little contact. I hope that you will make new friends where you are who will be better influences on your development as a young Catholic woman. Though I can understand you see her as a friend, she revealed herself to be a poor choice of friend for a girl with your potential. I will pray for you to find stable, moral Catholic friends in your new school.

Please write me again. I enjoyed hearing from you. Remember to pray the rosary each day for world peace and spiritual fortitude.

Yours truly,
Sister Paul

The first bookmark showed three children kneeling, hands together in prayer and a Virgin Mary floating before them in a blue haze—Our Lady of Lourdes. The second bookmark was older and when I looked at it, I realized it was more a prayer card than bookmark. The paper was yellowed and smelled like it had been in an old chest or attic for a long time. The picture was dark like the Stations of the Cross in St. John's church but St. Margaret of Antioch's tunic was brilliant red and the dragon under her foot had deep green scales, yellow teeth and a blue tongue falling out of its mouth onto the floor. I tossed the Prayers for Strong Families booklet into the closet; there was no mother here to pray for wisdom in raising her children or to obey her husband the way the faithful obey the Church. I spread the rosary, the bookmarks and prayer booklets, a Bible I'd found in my bedroom in New Orleans with Uncle Frank's name in it, two St. Anthony medals I'd had so long I didn't know where I'd gotten them, all across my bed. I hadn't expected Dad to mention church or go with me or even drop me off but I was surprised that Kiswana hadn't. She gave me books, she talked about school, she supervised our Saturday grocery making, she brought me Dessa to play with and when she talked about what The People needed, church and faith in God was always on her list but she never asked or even said she went to church herself. Sister Paul would say I could cure my loneliness by praying the rosary or going to Mass but I had always felt as lonely in church as out. No dead white Jesus, no matter how full of love, cared if girls didn't talk to me because they thought I thought I was better or could tell Shirleen she was wrong about me.

• • •

Before we pulled in the driveway, I leaned out the open car window to get the mail and lower the red flag. There were only a few envelopes, bills for Dad, and one for me from Shirleen. I felt happy and scared at the same time and it almost curdled my stomach but I ate everything at dinner so Dad wouldn't worry.

Dad went out to the barn and I went to the porch to read Shirleen's letter. It was nearly eight o'clock at night, the sky dark blue but still light enough to see even in most of the house without lamps. I thought I heard a motor some distance away, someone getting in a little extra work. I peeked around the house though I knew I didn't have to hide the letter from Dad. The big barn doors were open and a pile of rusted tools and weathered wood was in the grass nearby. I took my time and carefully peeled open the flap. Shirleen's handwriting was a lot like Sister Paul's, only loopier.

Dear Sandi,

Everyone here is fine. Auntie Z came through town for a few days and helped out with Dear. Did I tell you Dear has diabetes? No, I didn't because you haven't called. You told me you were out in the country. Does that mean there's no phones? I am sure Yolanda would like a call from you. I told her to write and gave her the envelope with your address on it so we'll see if she does. She needs to do something more than watching TV. At least she does her chores first now.

I'm glad your father is not leaving you alone too much yet. Being alone is something you WILL have to learn to deal with. A doctor is always busy and his first priority is his patients and oath, NOT his family. You will have to get to school on your own, do your homework on your own, and make friends yourself. You may need to get registered for school yourself, too. You should ask him as soon as you get this letter about school. I would hate to have all the education I paid for go to waste at some third-rate country school. I want you to be more than a secretary or someone's mother. I had plans and ambitions but I ended up with you and now it is too late.

I don't know why you are surprised that Louis Armstrong was poor. We're poor, too. You may have forgotten already but no matter how hard I work I will never make more money than I am making right now. Did you know Mother Dear owns this house? That she can kick us out anytime? That all the furniture is used? That we have a black and white TV while the welfare mother down the block with five kids has color? Every time I get in my car I hope it makes it where I'm going and back. All I ever do is work and take care of you and Yolanda. This is the real world here where people work and work to stay above water and never get anywhere or become anything. It may be hard to imagine now living with your father but you'd do best not to forget where you come from. There are more poor people in the world than rich. You may feel rich seeing people with no shoes but never think you are better because your father is a doctor and you look like a white person. Every time I let you out of the house, someone would think I was babysitting or your father was white. Do you know why the kids on the block and at school won't talk to you? Because of your superior attitude and your whiteness. None of that makes you better, Sandi. You need to get off your high horse or you will have no one in this world but your father who is always at work anyway.

I don't want to bad-mouth your father but it worries me that you are at the clinic all day. It's full of sick people, too many adults, and how can anyone keep track of you if they are so busy with sick people and babies? I'm sure you like living with your father, he is a soft touch, with you at least, but you need more supervision and I hope he realizes it before it is too late. He thinks you are the little girl he left and found again, but I know you better and I hope he sees you for what you are before it is too late. I don't want him sending you back because he couldn't control you or you're in trouble, and I know you know what I mean by that since you know everything you need to know about boys, like you told me. You decided to go which means you made that bed so lay in it. I can only support one child and have one here already.

Mother Dear, all your aunts and uncles and cousins, and Yolanda say hello. They hope you are well and happy.

Love,

your mama

I could barely read the end because my eyes were teary. I couldn't tell what I was feeling but most of it wasn't good. Dad called to me from the barn. I wiped my face, stuffed the letter in my back pocket and went over to help.

We gathered up garbage to burn; we were too far out for garbage trucks. We tossed into the oil drum behind the house newspapers, cellophane and cardboard from food boxes and meat, a worn-out toothbrush, dull razor blades, paper garbage, half-rotten wood. Dad squirted some lighter fluid into the drum, dropped in a match and a skinny flame jumped up, sank in then rose up again as several tall flames. Dad pulled me back a couple of feet. I took Shirleen's letter out of my pocket.

"Who's your letter from?" he said. I held it out to him. As he read it, his neck started to flush pink then red.

"I don't know what she's talking about," I said, feeling hot inside like the oil drum. "Hoping you 'see me for what I am,' what is that? She thinks I wanted that Champ bastard to follow me, she thinks I—Like she thinks I told Yolanda to come and just like she used to blame me if it was raining like I made it rain so she'd have to drop me off and be late for work which she never was 'cause she dropped me off before the nuns even got there. Why did I even write her? I mean, I leave, I finally leave and she still complains. I'm not even there! How can I make her mad when I'm not even there!" I thought of Sock It to Me and wanted to snap it in half and Shirleen, too.

"She has no right to talk to you that way," he said.

"She's my mother," I said, parroting Shirleen.

"Don't hold that against yourself." Dad gave me back the letter and I balled it up to throw it in the oil drum to burn with the rest of the trash. "You should write a rebuttal." He took the handle from a rusted hoe and churned the garbage. The flame shot up and died down again.

"What's that?" I said.

"An answer tearing apart your opponent's argument. Answer her point by point. She has no right to talk to you that way. Didn't you say *she* kept *you* inside? If she kept you inside, how can she say the kids on the block wouldn't play with you? You weren't given permission—like you need permission to play, you're . . . " We stared at the oil drum. One piercingly loud bug sounded off and when it stopped, we could hear a few crickets, the night bugs waking up as the sky got darker and darker blue, the eastern edge already dark purple and dotted with stars.

· · ·

Saturday, Miss Bettie stopped on her way past the nurses station to look at my hair, her hands skinny and gnarly like Mamalita's had been but even more gentle and hesitant, like I could be hurt or break, something I didn't feel any adult at home had ever thought.

"How's it looking, Miss Dixon?" Dad said, winking at me over her head. "You know I don't know anything about a girl's hair."

"The press still holding," she said, eyes tired and watery, "but the braids need redoing."

"Dessa can do it," I said.

Miss Bettie nodded. "C'mon by the house whenever, you always welcome, Sandrine," she said. Dad followed her down the hall.

"I'm going now," I said, grabbing the book I had on the counter.

Kiswana held the book down. "Wait and go back with Miss Bettie," she said in a Sister Mary Clare voice.

"No," I said, snatching the book so hard and fast Kiswana's hand slapped loudly on the counter, "I want to go now."

Kiswana followed me outside and watched me walk down the road. I turned before I went over the crest of the short hill and she was still there, arms folded against her white uniform. I thought, Go back inside, Shirleen.

The road was paved but it had been so dry the past month—I hadn't seen or heard more than ten minutes of rain since I'd gotten off the bus—it looked like a dirt lane. I stopped, thinking I heard steady traffic, low whistles, faint male voices saying things I couldn't understand. I looked ahead and back, saw no cars and started walking fast even though it was hot and sweat tickled my sides and back under my t-shirt. I got off the shoulder and walked in the grass, closer to the trees and bushes. At the bend between Dessa's and the hill near the clinic, the trees and bushes were thin and I stepped through them to what I thought would be thick trees and bushes scraggly from the trees getting all the light but it was all open space where trees had been cut. Rough stumps and splintered parts of trunks scattered from my feet to the hills in the distance, like thousands of men with axes were chopping their way through the county.

I ran the rest of the way to Dessa's, pausing on the driveway to slow down my heart.

. . .

Dessa stayed long enough to almost finish a game of pickup sticks. She had to walk back to go to the store with Miss Bettie and Susie.

It was quiet and Kiswana sat in the nurses' station, head on her fist, looking half-asleep. A baby cried in an exam room and Kiswana's head snapped up at the sound. She saw me and smiled. "Did Dessa go home?" she said.

"She had to help Miss Bettie."

I looked down the hall—Dad was in his office and Dr. Capdeau was leaning in the half-door of the pharmacy talking to Mr. Pradeesh. I still wasn't used to not filing, cleaning, answering phones—Kiswana had decided a couple weeks ago that I was not to work "hard" anymore so I rarely did anything except answer the phone for a few minutes or shake a test tube or two for Mrs. Feydeau and the one time Kiswana caught me with a broom sweeping the empty waiting room, she snatched the broom from my hands, not angry, just determined, and brought me more and more books which just filled my time because no one asked about them or what I thought, just saw me reading and gave a big smile or, like Mrs. Feydeau and some of the older women who came into the clinic, gave me a peppermint or a flower from a garden or a loose rhinestone. I was tired of books. I liked the biographies, histories and books of stories and poems but the other books kept telling me I was in love with white people and trying to be like them, that I didn't know what I already knew—that it was a white world and black people had to watch out for themselves, that a black person couldn't believe what white people said about them, just like a girl couldn't believe what men and boys said about her or said they thought or said they wanted and it was like school where everything was about boys, nothing about girls except a few randomly-placed insults.

I would've been tired of the house, too, if we were there long enough. On Sundays, Dad and I slept late and by the time we did laundry and cleaned the stinking leftovers out of the refrigerator, it was time for dinner and Monday again. I thought I missed Shirleen but I really missed Mamalita, someone to ask if I had a good day, to wake me up with What do you want to do today?, to hold my hand just because. Dad was there, he never yelled at me, he had paper taped to my door where he wrote down everything I read with a big smile but I was still, in a space deep in my chest next to my fading fear of men without eyes, very lonely.

· · ·

Another bag of books on the passenger seat. Dad heard my sigh. "What's the matter there, San?"

"Nothing." I wanted to say I was bored but I had no intention of going back to Shirleen so I kept my mouth shut though I couldn't think of anything to distract him from my sigh. I slumped in the seat and stared out the window, letting the trees, leaves and fence posts smear.

I felt hot inside. The first part of my rebuttal would be to tell Shirleen everything about Champ and the others who slowed down, looked, followed, whistled, smacked air kisses at me. But Shirleen might think I was bragging. And everything around me slowed as I remembered—I'd told Shirleen a car slowed down and men looked at me a long time; not looking up from her dinner plate, she said not to think I was cute, that it was just my color they saw. I couldn't tell then or now what she meant, if she was telling the truth or telling me I was ugly and only my color, or lack of, would get me attention.

I couldn't find a comfortable place in the house to sit. My bed was too soft and inside had gotten hot and would be until after dinner. I felt too exposed at the kitchen table, like Shirleen could swoop in and snatch the paper from me. I tried the porch next. It was cooler but I had to stack two legal pads together to keep the paper stiff enough to write on. Dad had told me to write my rebuttal a few times and not to send it until I thought it was ready. I didn't want to look at Shirleen's letter but I slowly unfolded it and took it one line at a time, writing answers like I would for a test in careful, complete sentences. When I finished the first page of her letter, I had two pages of sentences and my back and underarms were slick with sweat. I felt weak, teary, afraid and wanted to hide.

The barn was dark and the coolest place I'd felt aside from air conditioned places. The weakness started to fade. I smelled cigarette smoke and wet wood. Dad appeared from a corner with a rusted tool in each hand, one a sickle, the other a square-shaped shovel. He tossed them out the open door. He gave me a hug then I followed him to the corner and helped carry the old tools outside to the sun.

• • •

While I ate lunch, I stuck pickup sticks straight up in the dirt, digging the points into the red dirt until they stood in a circle all around me. It was the hottest day so far, the air felt like it could burn skin and the sun like it could go through bone but I still ate outside, needing a break from disinfectant, voices and air conditioning so high my toes inside my tennis shoes stayed cold. Outside it was quiet, like it was too hot for anything but me to move.

Kiswana came out with a paper sheet, her lunch and two Cokes, like she had every day. The bag of books she'd given me was behind me in the dirt; I carried it around but hadn't touched most of them since I put down *Twelve Years a Slave*. It gave me the shakes and my stomach was always flopped upside down.

"Who was this girl who gave you the note?" Kiswana said.

"The only friend I had at school." I felt like I was saying it with a six-year-old's tears and indignation but Kiswana didn't show anything. "She was just trying to help me protect myself."

"From what? Don't give me that you-couldn't-understand look." Kiswana finished a Coke before taking my note out of her pocket. "She's not inaccurate," she said. "She didn't say anything about pregnancy, though," she said.

"So?" I said.

"So?" Kiswana unwrapped her sandwich and stared right at me. I looked away, not wanting her to see anything about Lydia or Champ in my eyes. "What you most need to know is how not to get pregnant."

"I know that—stay away from penises."

Kiswana's back straightened. She opened her second Coke and took two sips, her eyes on me. "You can't stay away from them all your life. After you go to college, you'll want a husband, a strong black man to stick by you and take care of you and your kids and there's not only nothing wrong with that, it's essential to the—"

"Kiswana!" Mrs. Feydeau stood in the open clinic door. "You got that girl out in this heat again? Look at her." Mrs. Feydeau came closer, sweat breaking out over her upper lip and on her nose. "She looks like she's about to fall over. Come inside, baby, and cool off," she said, taking my arm. I did feel limp and heavy-lidded, the air almost too solid to breathe, and I let Mrs. Feydeau help me up and inside the chilled clinic.

"Frances?" Mrs. Feydeau said. "Don't you have some . . ."

Miss Frances set down the tray of test tubes and half-skipped over to the metal desk they shared, slid open the big file drawer and took out a plastic bag of ribbons, wide, thin, purple, gold, red, white, lime green, pink, striped. "I'm all ready," she said.

"No, you're busy, I'm the one ready," Mrs. Feydeau said. She took the bag of ribbons from Miss Frances who made a fake, big-lipped pout before she flashed me a smile. Mrs. Feydeau pointed me to the floor in front of the love seat they had people sit on to get blood drawn or wait for them to find a test result. I sat on the icy linoleum. Mrs. Feydeau took a comb, brush and a jar of yellow Ultra Sheen from her purse. When she sat behind me, she grabbed my shoulders and leaned close to my ear. "I've been waiting to do this since I saw you the first day," she said. She started undoing my fuzzy plaits. "Now just look at that face," she said to Miss Frances who smiled over her shoulder as she filled out forms. "That's a face that deserves some pretty hair. When I'm done, I'll give you a head scarf to wrap around it at night to keep it neat, okay?"

Miss Frances brought me magazines to read, *Ebony* and *Jet*, and a grocery bag half full of comic books—Superman, The Hulk, Justice League, Super Soul Comics and some with wide-eyed screaming people or laughing skulls on the front covers. "Every girl needs her light reading," Miss Frances smiled. Mr. Pradeesh called Miss Frances over to the pharmacy window and she added a week's worth of Jackson newspapers, three *Time* magazines and a *Life* magazine to my pile. I leaned back against Mrs. Feydeau's thighs. My skin finally cooled off.

Mrs. Feydeau used a ribbon to hold back most of my hair while she started individual braids near my neck. "Tell me," she said, "did your mama braid your hair much?"

"No."

I could feel Mrs. Feydeau waiting like a teacher for a student to give the rest of the answer but I said nothing else. Miss Frances looked over at us a moment and whatever look Mrs. Feydeau gave her made her tighten her mouth and gently shake her head. "Well," Mrs. Feydeau said, "Between me, Dessa, Frances and Miss Bettie, you will always look like a superstar. Lean forward a little bit so I can get at this kitchen."

• • •

Mrs. Feydeau encouraged me to eat in Dad's office and nap each day after lunch. She brought me more of what Kiswana called "junk" to read—more comic books though they were boy stuff all about superheroes, *Seventeen*, *Glamour*, *Vogue*, *Harper's Bazaar*. I glanced at the pictures, pausing if Beverly Johnson or the other black model appeared in a spread but I didn't read much. It was good to be bored. When I got too bored, I worked on my rebuttal. I thought of showing it to Dad but I wanted it to be good enough first.

• • •

Dear Mama,

I still haven't heard from Yolanda but I did get a letter from Sister Paul. She wished me luck in my new school and told me to pray the rosary every day.

I know what you meant about the phone. You meant I haven't called you. Dad gave you the number and I sent it in the letter I wrote you and you haven't called me. You could have given Yolanda the number already. And is Yolanda really doing the chores? I had to force her just to do a little bit and then when school started she took so long with homework I had to do it all myself just to get it done unless I had homework to do because you think my day has more hours in it than anyone else's.

Living here is not the first time I have ever been alone and being in Meridian with Dad and Philipa and

Yolanda wasn't the first time either. Even in New Orleans with you I was alone. I walked to school myself, got through the whole day by myself, walked home myself, and until you got home I cleaned up the house even if it looked clean so you wouldn't come in complaining that you had already worked all day and now had to work all night and I never remember you working all night at anything, except looking at TV or talking on the phone or bouncing on the bed with Raheem and Ray Ray and Joe Henry and that pervert Champ or sitting on the sofa thinking of what else I needed to do for you. I did my homework myself. I walked myself to church. When cars slowed down and scared me into thinking something would happen to me, I figured out on my own to walk against traffic and down one-way streets. All you had to say when I told you about that was Stop bragging and It's just your color they see. So I was always alone. At least Dad has a reason, a job to do that keeps him away. You were sitting right across from me <u>and</u> somewhere else. You always treated me like a bad person, like a pest, so you want to think Dad is teaching me all about being alone and lonely but I learned all about that from <u>you</u>.

You said you ended up with me like it was my fault. I may not know much but I do know that babies don't ask to be born or pick their parents because if they did I'd have to say I made the wrong choice. Now that I'm out of your way, you can go on with whatever it is you want to do with your life—buy a new car, get married again, move in with Dear and give her her medicine, quit work and go on welfare so you can have a color TV, you can do anything you want now because you don't have me around. And without you around, I can play with kids, go to school without worrying what you might hear and beat me for, don't have to hear you telling me kids hate me because I am the wrong shade of brown instead of the truth, that they hate me because you won't let me near them. I'll be riding the bus with kids and I'm even going to stay after school and do something so I can be around them more. You confused your hate for me with kids hating me.

I never thought I was white or better. The girls at school and you thought that but none of you ever asked me what I thought or wanted or felt and if you had you would've known that to me white people are like aliens. I see them at school, at stores when I was allowed to go to any, on TV when I was allowed to watch any and I must have been the only straight-A student at school not allowed to watch TV, and I never felt like they had anything to do with me. I saw Dad talking to a white man the other day and it hit me I haven't seen more than ten white people since I got off the bus.

And dad is <u>not</u> rich. He works at a clinic for poor people and I heard the nurses talking about how the state wasn't sending enough money to buy all they need and pay everybody a fair wage. The house we are in has one bathroom and the richest thing about it is it is on a lot of land, most of the land Dad leases out to some farmers. We have less in our refrigerator than you and Yolanda do. And nobody here, even though everybody knows my Dad is one of the doctors, thinks I'm a stuck-up yellow bitch. All I ever tried to do was keep you happy and not get beaten and all you do is complain, even when I am finally out of your house and not your responsibility anymore and no longer your overwhelming, undeserved burden.

You say you don't want to bad-mouth Dad but you enjoy it and always did. Just like with me. You saw Champ and just knew I'd asked him to put my hand in his pants. I wanted to throw up. When I saw you I thought you would save me but instead you beat me because you have always thought I was bad because you never looked at the me in front of you. Even if his hands had been covered in my blood and he was holding my intestines in his hands, you would've beaten me for being this bad, evil girl you want Dad to think I am, an ten-year-old after her twenty-five-year-old mother's so-called friend. Aunt Margie told me the truth. I will never be some fourteen-year-old pretending to be twenty-two so she can drink and get pregnant. I know enough about men to know I don't want anything to do with them forever. I wish I could or ever could have talked to you. I was scared. And I was all by myself. Absolute strangers have been more mother to me than you have. Sister Paul loves me more than you do. Sister Lawrence's eyes got wet when I told her the one person I was sure loved me, Mamalita, died. You never had a word to say. You never even told me you were sorry she died. You never mentioned it again like her dying was the same as sweeping cigarette butts off the porch, done, out of sight out of mind. It was nothing to worry yourself about because it only had to do with me and anything to do with me is less important than dirt.

Don't worry about me coming back. Why go back to a woman who would rather have any other child in the world than her own? Now I know why you wouldn't let me play with kids on the block or at school and why you were always so mad and nervous when Dad came to get me. Because you were afraid they'd be nice to me and I'd wonder why you weren't. Because you were afraid I'd tell them you never did anything for me. As long as I can remember I've made my bed, my breakfast, done my own hair, helped myself with homework, cleaned your house and even with straight As didn't get to see TV or movies or get more than one thing for Christmas because you knew that I would see what it was like to be liked and wanted instead of hated and you thought I'd come back one day realizing what you are and I did. Aunt Margie told me all about you. You never took care of anybody. Carina did and she's gone forever because of you just like me.

Don't bother writing me either. I burned your last letter in the trash and I'll burn all the rest. It should make you happy to throw me away like you always wanted but didn't because you were afraid what other people would think.

Sandrine Miller

• • •

I didn't show the letter to Dad. I addressed an envelope, wishing I could scotch the address from my memory. On the way out the driveway, I put it in the mailbox and raised the flag. All day I felt like I still had to finish it then I felt like it would still be in the mailbox, God stopping me from sending it. Dessa and I sat in Dad's office, Dessa braiding my hair and me reading to her. When I read a word she wasn't sure about, the comb or her fingers would stop so I could explain. Later I walked home with her. I saw Susie on the front steps sewing but she didn't look up and Dessa said to pay her no mind.

When we got home, the red flag was down and the letter

gone. I swallowed past a rock in my throat thinking that in a few days, Shirleen would get the letter, open it, read it and scream at the letter like it was me standing in front of her. Dad made squash with onions and showed me how he poked the squash with the spoon to see if it was done, something I hadn't thought of. We also hadn't thought of what to eat with it so just had squash and some bread.

The reception on the TV was bad that night so the Wednesday night movie was full of snow and everything the people said ended with hisses and crackles. Dad said we needed a checkerboard. We went outside to look at stars. I realized Shirleen and the letter were in the back of my mind when I was surprised there were no streetlights. Stars powdered the sky. The only star I knew about was the North Star and that was from books. I stepped off the porch into the semi-darkness in front of the house to look for the North Star, lights from the house around me on the grass.

"I'll never tell you you can't see her," Dad said. I knew he was talking about Shirleen and I didn't turn around. "When Mama finally started getting you for the summers, when you were three . . . after that I noticed you were two girls, the smiling, laughing girl at Mamalita's was a quiet girl with big watching eyes with her mother. I thought she'd made you scared of me."

I felt like he was talking to himself but I knew he meant it for me. I sat next to him on the edge of the porch and lay against his arm, hugging it tight, the nasty air in my stomach slowly leaking out, and I felt something I'd never felt before—small but safe.

Many thanks to Elizabeth Dewberry, The Pirate's Alley Faulkner Society, Inc./ The William Faulkner–William Wisdom Creative Writing Competition 2006, and, especially, Elizabeth Clementson and Robert Lasner, who supported this book after completion and made publication possible.

Many more thanks to Derek for reading multiple drafts and always believing in this book and me.